WALKING IN HER SHADOW COPY

THE PSYCHOSIS EDITION

DAVID PARKER-ROSS

TAIRIS ANDERS MEDIA, LLC

COPYRIGHT

WALKING IN HER SHADOW BY DAVID PARKER-ROSS

Editor Tegan Bourke
Ebook and Paperback art by: Angela Stevens
Hardback art by Lara Wynter
Audiobook Read by Tegan Bourke

EBook 978-1-959138-18-1
Paperback 978-1-959138-19-8
Hardback 978-1-959138-20-4

Facebook.com/DavidParkerRoss
Contact@JennaPlural.com

ALSO BY DAVID PARKER-ROSS

ALL TITLES AVAILABLE ON AUDIO

Perceptions – The Rise of Jenna Plural
<u>Jenna Plural Wants You</u>
<u>That Girl from Wagga</u>
<u>Walking in Her Shadow</u>
<u>Awakening of Hannah Grant</u>
<u>The Angel of Phobos</u>
Memoir of a Martian (Out November 2023)
The Cult of Artemis Bailey
<u>The Rise of Artemis: The Golden Age Edition</u>
The Amazon Chronicles
<u>Miss Eve and the City of Men</u>

DEDICATION

For the world's greatest nephew
Jaxson Collins

Buddy, as I write this dedication, you are not yet one year old, and we have not even met in person. But your amazing smile brightens my day, and I look forward to every time your parents post pictures of you.

Right now, this book means little more to you than something interesting to chew on. Indeed, due to its content, you really should be an adult before trying to read it. By that time, I will be extremely old and senile or dead. So I wanted to say do not be confused about why I dedicated a book to you about a psychotic serial killer. It was simply the book I wrote the year this world saw your arrival.

All my love goes with you, Jaxson, on your journey through this crazy thing called life.

Uncle David
22nd October 2022

AUTHOR'S NOTE

Perceptions is a series that tells tales from different characters' perspectives. Each has their own ideas, their own values, their own beliefs, and their own memories.

The characters, including the narrator, have their own perception of the events that took place at the time of the stories. They may very well have political, religious, and social opinions. Those opinions do not necessarily reflect this author or anyone involved with the creation of this work. Indeed I have very much tried to keep my personal opinions out of the stories.

The whole idea is to leave it to you, the reader, to make up your mind on the rights and wrongs of the characters within the tales.

Memory is a fickle beast; not everyone will remember events similarly. One should not assume that a narrator is either accurate or, for that matter, even truthful.

Perceptions... It's all about who you believe.

Clear Skies to You,
David Parker-Ross

WALKING IN HER SHADOW

BY EMMA DODGSON

Dedication
Jenna Plural
My heart, my soul, my leader, the Future

From the private files of Lieutenant Emma Dodgson (Deceased)

I f you're either reading this or listening to this, then I am dead.

Hopefully, it was at the age of eighty-nine with my wife at my side and grandchildren playing in the yard. However, I somehow doubt it. If my demise was premature, then I hope I did shuffle off this mortal world in some manner befitting a Marine. I hope that my name is etched on some plaque somewhere amongst the honored dead, and that my friends and companions remember me with fondness.

Many people will not agree with the decisions I've made, but that's more indicative of weakness in our society, where most people don't have what it takes to do what is necessary.

I make no apologies for my actions, and I'm frankly quite proud of them. I hope that, as you read this journal, you'll agree with me. But since many will not and potentially will come after me for my actions, this'll stay locked away in a computer file designed automatically to be released upon the recording of my death.

I am an unrepentant patriot, and that's something you'll just simply have to deal with. Before its fall, America was the greatest country in the world. Despite my loyalty to the new Solar Confederation being without question, I will always be an American. I will always be a proud United States Marine, and hope that I played a part in restoring her greatness once again.

However, this story isn't about that. It's about the rise of the greatest leader the human race has ever known. And the small part I played in assisting her rise.

Lieutenant Emma S. Dodgson, MOV.

March 12th, '98

CHAPTER ONE

THE DAY IT ALL BEGAN

My story begins in my hometown of Sedona, Arizona, although I was raised in South Carolina until I was seventeen and Papa retired from the Navy. I joined the United States Marines straight out of high school. I didn't have the grades for college, so military service was the only option available to me. Having said that, the Marines are the only division of the military that you can't be called up for and you have to apply to. I did. I applied three times before I was accepted. I'm not exactly an athlete. I'm small and appear ineffectual in most people's eyes, and it was quite a struggle to get through the physical rigors of the selection process. To my surprise, and probably everyone else's, I finally managed it, and the day eventually came when I had to set off to begin my basic training. I took the bus from Arizona to Illinois. I know it was silly. No-one takes buses these days other than tourists, and it even costs more than a plane, due to the lack of demand. However, I'd never left Sedona before. Well, unless you include trips into Phoenix and the surrounding area. Which I don't.

It was a good chance to see America before I left it. For the most part, I enjoyed it; however, staying in the seedy motels was most disconcerting when we stopped overnight. I headed out to buy cleaning supplies and bed sheets within minutes of seeing my room. I spent several hours cleaning it and changing the laundry before going to bed. What made it even worse, was that I heard the couple in the room next to me either fucking or having some seriously wild dreams.

I only slept for a few hours and almost missed the bus leaving the next morning. I missed breakfast, which always made me cranky, so instead of reading, as I had for most of the journey, I curled up against the window and went to sleep. I slept for several hours and was quite annoyed, having paid all this money, and yet missing half of the greatest country that ever existed.

As we moved further north, the weather turned bleak, and it wasn't fun anymore. I didn't want to look out at the dreary sky and gloomy streets. When we finally rolled into Chicago, it was even worse. It was a nasty little town that appeared to only invest money in its tall, ugly skyscrapers. Fortunately, I wasn't going to be staying there, and I made myself look out across Lake Michigan on the other side of the bus. We eventually reached our terminus, and my fellow passengers and I wearily traipsed off the vehicle.

It was several more miles to get to the United States Marine training ground, where I was to begin my eleven weeks of basic training. I knew it was going to be tough. As I've told you, I made three attempts to join, and barely passed when I finally did. I was exceedingly nervous about whether I would make it through. It would be most humiliating, were I to fail and have to return home to my father, who was annoyed I didn't follow in his footsteps and join the Navy.

I got a cab the rest of the way. A modern one that traveled much faster than the old-fashioned bus. In less than ten minutes, I was standing outside the front gates with my bag over my shoulder and excitement in my heart.

I walked to the guard post, where two Marines were chatting, not noticing my approach.

"Excuse me, S...S...Sir," I said nervously, my stammer more obvious than usual. The Marine looked up at me. "I'm a new Marine here to st...st...start my b...b...basic training."

It startled me how fast he moved out of the cabin. He strode right up to me and pressed his face so close into mine that I stepped back, but he just stepped forward.

"Stand still!" He barked, and I complied. "You, Miss, are not a Marine!" he screamed into my face.

"B...b... but..." I replied, confused.

"*Did I ask you to speak?!*" He was so shrill now that his voice disappeared, as he reached the end of the sentence.

"N...N....No, Sir."

"Get this into your tiny head, Missy!" He jabbed me hard on the side of my head with his finger – hard enough to actually hurt. "You are nothing! You have to earn the right to call yourself a United States Marine! *Have you earned that right?!*"

I started to feel annoyed. Not at him. He was just doing his job but at me for letting this situation intimidate me. "N...N...No, Sir."

"Can't you speak properly, recruit? Are you mentally challenged? Do we need to put you down? Are we having learning difficulties?"

I concentrated very hard to get the words out and blurted successfully, "No, Sir." Which literally answered all of his questions. My very pronounced stutter was not the result of nerves, although most believed that to be the case. It was the result of a brain injury I had incurred when I was seven, and my father threw me against the mantlepiece in our living room. It may have been prevented had they sought medical attention at the time, but the damage became permanent and incurable.

The Gunnery Sergeant pointed down the pathway toward the main building, where I saw many Marines parading up and down in various stages of their training. There was also a small group of people standing in civilian clothes. "That is where you are supposed to be."

I made to move in that direction, but he stepped in front of me. "Did I say you could move?"

"N...N...No, Gunnery Sergeant."

"What is your name?"

"Emma Dodgson."

"That is 'Emma Dobson, *Sir!*'" The last two words were positively shrill.

"E...Emma *Dodgson*, Sir." I said, emphasizing the correction of my last name.

He reached his hand out towards the other Marine, who had come up to join us while we were conversing. A man of a lower rank – which I can't recall – handed him a tablet. He scrolled a finger down it, and I assume he was checking my name off. He handed it back to the other man and stood upright with his hands by his sides.

"Get moving, Dobson!"

I wanted to correct his use of my name again but thought better of it, and I turned and started walking towards the main building. However, I found him walking along just behind me.

"Pick those feet up, Dobson." I walked faster. "Run, Dobson." I started to run, but I guess it wasn't good enough as he screamed, "Faster, Dobson!" And I realized he was running behind me. As we reached the group who were attempting to stand at attention, he screamed at me one last time. "Throw your pack down over there and fall into line!"

He pointed to where an array of bags were piled up, and I moved swiftly and dropped it amongst them, and then I joined the end of the line next to a tall gaunt man. The Gunnery Sergeant went over to another Sergeant and talked to him quietly. The other man looked up at me, and a deep scowl crossed his face. "Is there something over here that interests you, recruit?" he shouted.

"N...n...no, Sir." Someone in my line of recruits snorted in laughter, probably at my speech impediment. The Sergeant shouted over at me.

"Your eyes will stay faced front, and you will not move them, or yourself, until you are told to! Am I clear?"

"Yes, Sergeant," I replied, pleased I said it clearly.

"Louder!" He shouted

"Yes, S...s...Sergeant." Fuck and double damn!

He moved away, and I felt a sense of relief as I stopped being the center of attention. We weren't allowed to speak and had to remain standing until they unceremoniously led us into the quartermaster's to get our gear. It was like a production line. The person behind the counter would shout out, asking for your size, and you got shirts, pants, boots, and so on.

We were then led into another room. We were made to line up along a white line. Just standing there, holding our kit in our arms. Then, he gave us the order to change. I hesitated. While there were several other women, it was mostly men, and even those giving the orders were men. As the others rapidly stripped off their clothes, the Sergeant saw me staring uncomfortably at them. He marched over to me, and with what would be normal for my next eleven weeks, he got into my face. "Did you hear my order?!"

"Y...y...yes, Sergeant."

"Do you know how to put on a uniform?!"

"Yes, S...Sergeant."

"So, why aren't you doing it?!"

I glanced down the line at the naked bodies around me. Despite society having finally achieved equality, I was raised in a devoutly religious family, and there were certain things we didn't do.

"Men, Sergeant." I don't know why I was being such an ass about this. Although I hadn't thought about it, this was obviously going to happen.

"Oh dear, are we shy?!" he shouted into my face. I was going to get tired of this extremely fast. "The United States Marine Corps is an equal opportunity organization. We don't care if you are male or female, gay or straight, black or white, or green and blue. You will get changed now, or I'll ask some of these *men* to help you do it. Are we clear?"

I nodded and said, "Yes, Sergeant."

As I removed my clothing, I tried to fight back the tears of anger. I believe I succeeded because, had it been seen, I'm sure the drill sergeant's wrath would have been down upon me again. I kept my eyes closed as I changed, only to open them when I absolutely had to. I didn't want to see the others looking at me. However, I heard a man speak beside me as I pulled off my shirt. "What the fuck?!"

I opened my eyes and looked at him, almost in a panic. I assumed he was looking at my breasts, but realized instead that he was looking at the scars on my back. I hastily pulled on my uniform shirt and turned away from him.

Because of my delay, I was the last to finish, and of course, that drew more screams and shouts at me. I endured them.

Eventually, we were led to another room, where we were made to line up in a queue outside a door. Three at a time, recruits were sent in, and I heard the buzz, and dreaded it. United States Marines were allowed to grow their hair long and have it tied up, but not in basic training. My long brown hair that had taken me years to grow down my back was about to depart. When my turn came, I entered. There were three barber seats, and as we went in, three recruits jumped up with newly shaved heads, and we took their places, and my long hair fell from my head. I wondered if I had bitten off more than I could chew. But no, I wanted to be a proud Marine, damn it. I wanted to fight the enemies of America. Whatever hell I was going to go through, it was my destiny to serve as a United States Marine.

My head felt cold as we ran from the barbers to the next room, where we were issued our rifles. We were then taken on to where we were to be billeted. There were no assigned bunks. We just took the one that lined up with where we stopped in line, as we ran to the end of the room. I was about halfway down, and I took the opportunity to glance around, hoping that those on either side of me would be female. One was, and the other wasn't. We stood at the end of the beds as the drill sergeant walked up and down in front of us. He went through what would happen during this first week and told us to prepare our kits for inspection.

As the Sergeant left us alone, there was a collective sigh of relief, and the small buzz of conversation started.

"Hey there." I turned to see a short dark girl with a nice smile and perky cheeks. "I'm Lydia."

"Emma, n...n...nice to meet you," I replied as we started sorting out our kit, and I wondered what had happened to the belongings that I had brought with me. I was not to see them again until the end of training.

"Nice to meet you, too, Emma. I'm from El Paso. Where are you from?"

"She's from Dumb Ass." A man I would come to know as Randall, said from the bunk opposite. He was a complete pig of a man. Of course, I didn't know him then, and

I stared at him incredulously at his comment, as he folded up a pair of pants.

"Is it really n...n...necessary for you to be uh...uh...offensive?" I said, causing both him and several others to laugh.

"Oh my God, can you hear her?" he laughed patronizingly. "I hear there's always one dumbass in every boot camp. I think we've found ours." There were more laughs at my expense.

"Leave her alone," Lydia chided gently. "We are all in this together."

"That's total bullshit," he said sneeringly. "There are always those that shouldn't have got passed selection that holds everyone else back. She couldn't even get onto the campground without causing problems. She's going to be responsible for bringing down the team."

"That's n....n...not really fair. You haven't even given me a chance yet," I said, hoping that I would be able to reason with him, but he just sneered at me.

"You can't even talk properly. Just do yourself and us a favor, and quit before you drag us all down with you."

I couldn't help but blush and look away, my embarrassment mixed with my anger, as I finished unpacking my kit. Had it not been for him distracting me, I probably wouldn't have made such a mess of it. Ten minutes later, I got another bawling out in front of everybody. Again, doubts started to slip into my head. However, I already knew Randall Alice would be a problem that needed dealing with, and I had long known how to deal with problems like him.

CHAPTER TWO

THE BULLY

"Come on, Emma, you can do it!" As I lay in the mud, barely able to move, I didn't believe Lydia's words of encouragement. "Move it! Before the sergeant sees you," she said when I still didn't respond. My body ached, and I was tired of all the shit that was going on in this new life.

We were only three weeks into it, and the thought of eight more was more excruciating than the pain that wracked my body. The wet mud was sucking me down, making it virtually impossible to shimmy along with my elbows as I was supposed to. I put in a final effort, deciding that I would give up if I didn't succeed.

The suction beneath me made it all the harder to lift my body, but I made it. I moved out from under the barbed wire and started to get up on all fours to stand up. A boot came down on my neck, pushed my face back into the wet mud. It lifted off me almost as soon as it came. I managed to lift my head slightly and saw the back of Randall as he raced on, having overtaken me. Lydia shouted some expletives after him. She then turned back to me and grabbed my elbow to help me up. I snatched it away aggressively, snarling.

"I don't n...n...need help."

She just stared at me. "Fuck you, Emma. I hung back to help you at the cost of my own time count. I've tried to be your friend, but you don't make it easy."

With that, she raced ahead and jumped up the climbing wall behind Randall. Then the voice we all feared came from behind me.

"Get on your feet, Dobson!" The sergeant screamed. "What do you think this is? Naptime?"

I scrambled up as best I could. I looked back to where the sergeant had come from. I knew that there was no way that he hadn't see what Randall had just done to me. I had no time to ponder it further as he chased me up to the wall. Fortunately, I managed to clear it without much of a struggle. At the top, I looked back down at the sergeant, who was now shaking his head patronizingly at me.

Later that day, I saw the Sarge and Randall laughing and chatting together, and even though I couldn't hear them and they never looked in my direction, I knew they were talking about how to get rid of me. The motherfuckers were clearly conspiring to take away my dreams to play my part in the war and give those Peon fucker's some payback from Uncle Sam.

This intimidation continued until the fifth week, when the final insult happened. Our furlough had been canceled because I had failed to complete a course in the allotted time, and they applied the 'if one fails, all fail' rule.

The abuse was full-on that night.

11

I was called names that do not bear repeating. I just sat on my bed and took it. However, the furlough was reinstated the next day, and we all got ready to go out for the night. We were not allowed to leave until our uniforms were clean and pristine. I had made sure mine was perfect. I wanted to get away from this place for the night, not with the others, but just out on my own.

I was in the bathroom when it happened. I was checking that I looked respectable in the mirror when someone came in and grabbed me from behind. I just managed to see in the reflection that it was Randall, before he spun me around and pushed me into a toilet stall. I tried to implement my training, but he quickly countered my move. Holding my arm behind my back, he pushed my head down into the toilet – which he hadn't flushed, but I'm not about to describe what was in there. He placed his knee upon my back and held me down as he flushed the toilet, and the water swirled and splattered into my face and onto my clothing.

"Give it up, Rapunzel, or this just gets worse." He released me and left. I fell to the floor and lay there spitting water. I climbed onto my knees and heaved violently into the bowl several times. I turned around on the floor, shut the door with my feet, and hugged my knees to my chin.

No! I wasn't going to put up with this anymore. I knew what to do with bullies. I had dealt with that bitch Brenda Moffat who had tormented me in High School about my stammer. To this day, they've never found her body.

It would take several days to come up with a plan, and I started to purloin items that would be of use to me. I studied my quarry carefully, but Randall was hardly ever alone. The Sarge, on the other hand, now that was a different matter. I learned that he would go drinking in the NCO's mess after we were locked down for the night. So I had to wait for another furlough. I could hardly risk sneaking out after lights out!

It was a Thursday when the opportunity came along. No-one was concerned that I wasn't going with them.

I stayed in the billet as everyone left.

Nobody waited for me, not even Lydia, who had given up on her attempts to be friends with me. I didn't know what I had done wrong. I didn't care. When silence fell in the billet, I got up and took a long shower, scrubbing my face until it was red raw. I then got a fresh uniform, or rather the one I'd been wearing that day. It was certainly cleaner than the one I had prepared for the night out. I collected some things that I needed and headed out into the night.

I headed to the NCO's mess and ensured no-one was watching me. I found the drill sergeant's open-topped Jeep, climbed into the back, and lay on the floor patiently.

It wasn't as if I had a great plan. I didn't even know how long I'd have to wait, or even where the sergeant would go when he came out.

I lay there for almost two hours, not moving until I heard people coming and going, and even talking right near the Jeep.

Eventually, the sergeant came out, and I recognized his voice, even though the liquor slurred his speech. His friend was trying to persuade him not to drive, but he just laughed it off, climbed in, and started up the engine. As we started to move off, I took a gamble and looked out from underneath my blanket. I could see we were heading up the road toward the base's exit. We weren't traveling fast, for he clearly liked being in control of his vehicle, and he didn't switch on the automated systems that would allow it to drive itself.

We headed out into the streets, and I waited until we turned a few bends before I moved. You may think it's stupid that I made my move while traveling about forty miles an hour, and it probably was, but I didn't want to end up somewhere we could be seen and lose my chance.

I pulled out the length of wire I'd taken from the base and curled the ends around my hands as I climbed up into the seat behind him. He didn't even look up into his mirror. I reached over his head and pulled it taut against his neck. He never even saw it coming. I yanked it tight, but I knew his physical strength would be greater than mine, so I twisted the ends around the back of the headrest.

I kept twisting as he clawed at his neck, and seconds later, we went off the road. I was thrown from the Jeep as it tipped onto its side, and I rolled down a small embankment on the side of the road. Apart from a couple of scrapes and bruises, I was unharmed, and I got up. I turned back to the Jeep, which was tipped up on its passenger side. He was still tied to the headrest and hung down to where his feet barely touched the ground.

It was quick for him, for his neck snapped when the vehicle had turned over. I untied the wire and lowered him to the ground. I then reached down and opened the hood.

It was a little bit of a struggle getting it to open, but I could reach in enough to wiggle the coolant wires until they came away. I then turned on the engine again, as it had turned off automatically in the event of the accident. It hummed to life once more.

With my hands in my pockets, I started walking back to the base, humming 'America the Beautiful.' I was about halfway there when, behind me, the Jeep exploded. I looked back to see a tiny mushroom cloud go up into the night sky as the reactor overheated. My one disappointment was he never saw me, and he never knew who did it to him.

I slept well that night, and we even got an extra hour to lie in as the sergeant failed to report for duty and wake us up.

Fortunately, a car reactor overheating doesn't leave much of the body for a decent autopsy, and in time, it was concluded that he'd died in a drunk driving accident. Everyone was a little shocked at the death of our sergeant, and the fact that we got the next few days off of training made everyone in my billet very happy.

I wanted to tell them they had me to thank for it, but I doubt they would've believed me. The next two weeks went a lot smoother. Even Randall laid off me for a while, and I think that's because we got a new drill sergeant to replace his bestest buddy. Damn! Even as I write this, I get so angry. I was too good to both of them. I didn't make them suffer.

However, I started to enjoy my training, and slowly, I started to improve. I enjoyed the hand-to-hand combat best, for I imagined looking into a Peon's face, and he would look into my eyes at the American who was about to dispatch him to Hell. Even my body started to become accustomed to the vigorous torture. Which, I suppose, was the point.

With graduation coming up fast, I could've let Randall off the hook. The chances of us being posted to the same unit in the solar system were slim to none. However, there was a principle at stake here. He had wanted to ruin my chances to serve my country, and if you think about that, it's not behavior becoming of a United States Marine. It was without honor. So, all in all, I'd be doing America a favor by taking him out so that he couldn't dishonor a proud legacy.

Finding an opportunity proved most vexing, and it seriously looked like he would get away without receiving his overdue punishment.

Graduation day finally came, and I had made it. Barely. Parents began arriving, and I looked out eagerly to find mine. I'd really hoped they would come. I wanted them to be proud of me, but unfortunately, I was to be disappointed, and I watched as mothers and fathers, brothers and sisters, gushed over their precious offspring in their dress uniforms. When the new Marines had the opportunity to show their family around in a more relaxed atmosphere, I returned to my billet, sat on my bed, and read.

I was surprised when someone came in. I was not expecting anybody. Especially not Randall, who came up to his bed opposite mine. I tried to ignore him, but there was new ammunition to fire at me.

"Wow, Rapunzel, even your parents hate you, don't they?" He chuckled as he opened his locker to get something. Of course, I didn't rise to his juvenile bait and simply ignored him. "Don't you even have a boyfriend to come see you graduate?" This made me think of my high school sweetheart, who I'd been with for several years. I'd broken it off when I'd been accepted into the Marine Corps. I so missed Calvin. I didn't respond to Randall and continued to ignore him.

"Nah, you're probably still a virgin?" He laughed, finding himself most amusing. I simply turned the page, but I wasn't actually reading now. "You know, I could fix that for you." I slowly raised my eyes toward him and gave him a disgusted look. He just laughed. "Nah, just kidding. I'd have to be pretty desperate to wanna fuck you. You'll probably get captured on your first mission and pop your cherry with a dozen sex-starved Peons. They don't care who they fuck."

I had finally had enough.

"You are the m....m...most uncouth and vulgar man I have ever met, P...Private Alice," I said softly. "You are a d...disgrace to that uniform you wear."

That was possibly the worst thing you could say to a Marine; however, he had pushed all my buttons.

His grinning face turned angry, and he stepped forward, raising the back of his hand to me. I didn't move. I just sat there and smiled, knowing that the strike would end with him in the stockade and possibly a dishonorable discharge. Unlike the toilet incident, he ran the risk of leaving a mark. He paused as he realized this and lowered his hand, sneering, "You're not worth it, Rapunzel." He turned away and headed to the bathroom. "See you in hell, bitch."

As the bathroom door shut behind him, I carefully closed my book and gently laid it aside. I got up and opened the drawer beside my bunk. I lifted my cotton briefs, picked up the combat knife I kept for such an opportunity, and slipped it into my belt.

Gently humming 'My Country 'Tis of Thee', I headed to the bathroom. I opened the door and stepped in. I looked under the gap beneath the doors of each cubicle until I found him. I felt a little guilty at the indignity of what was about to happen. His trousers around his ankles, sitting on the john would be a most undignified way to go out of this world.

Of course, the cubicle was locked, but it wasn't exactly designed to keep some criminal element out. I stepped away from it, took a quick step forward, and slammed my boot against the door. It flew open, and he sat there, looking up at me, the epitome of startled. He scrambled to gather his pants.

I stepped up to him quickly, grabbed a handful of his hair, and slammed his head back against the cistern behind him. Before he could recover, I slammed his head back several times until he was too groggy to retaliate effectively.

"Rapunzel," he moaned barely audibly. I kept smashing his head back until I was sure he was no immediate threat. I then pushed the cubicle door shut and had to force it in place due to the damage I had done.

I then stood with my legs on either side of his and held his head back by gripping a mop of his red hair in my clenched fist. I smiled down at him as he stared up at me with unfocused eyes, trying to gather his senses. When he made to speak again, I just spat into his mouth. I wanted desperately to do this slowly, take my time to enjoy it, and make it as painful and degrading as possible. After all, you surely can't disagree with me that he didn't deserve it.

A moment of panic suddenly overcame me when I heard the main door of the bathroom opening, followed by footsteps. As I turned my head to look in that direction, Randall took advantage of the situation and suddenly tried to push me off him. I quickly sat down on his lap, facing him as I pulled my knees together against his thighs to stop him from kicking out. I jammed my left arm against his throat, and pushing hard, held my other hand over his mouth. I felt a little grossed out as I felt his exposed genitalia pressed against me, but I was compelled to tolerate it. I even think he got a little aroused as I sat there, but that could have been my imagination in very uncomfortable circumstances.

I heard whoever entered the bathroom pause outside our cubicle, and I pushed harder against the asshole's throat to ensure his silence. I kept looking back over my shoulder, wondering what I'd do if this someone noticed the broken lock. I had no idea if there was any damage visible on the outside. I looked back at Randall, whose eyes were bulging from the sockets with his restricted air. The footsteps outside moved away, and moments later, I could hear someone urinating against the metal of a urinal. Randall made one last ditch effort to cry out, but I just leaned into the arm I had against his windpipe. I put my cheek against his whispered, barely audibly, "Shush, p...please don't make this d...difficult." I slightly released his throat. Just enough for him to get his breath before reapplying pressure. I know I could have dispatched him in this way, but I wasn't really satisfied with that. I was taking a big risk while someone else was in the bathroom. It just wasn't right to end this quite so quickly. I waited impatiently as I heard the interloper washing his hands. There was another moment of tension as I heard the footsteps stop outside my cubicle. However, much to my delight and the terror of Randall, the man left the bathroom.

I smiled down at him.

"Relax," I said soothingly as I gently ran my fingers gently through his hair. "You n... need to be honest with yourself and admit you know you've b...been asking for this," I said gently and somewhat seductively. "You r...really only have yourself to blame. I'm not doing this b...because I want to, Randall. I'm d...doing this because I have n...n...no choice. You really are a disgrace to that uniform." He went to try to speak again, but I lifted a finger to my lips. "No, no, no, Randall, don't spoil this m...moment for me with your excuses."

Scrounging together a last bit of effort, he made to lunge at me once more, and again, I banged his head back into the cistern several times until he was almost senseless. I sighed, looking down at him again, this time with disappointment. "You really are a bad b...boy Randall. Don't you think you should try to maintain some d...dignity in this situation? I feel so very embarrassed for you."

I started to sing to him softly, like a mother comforting a child.

"My country 'tis of thee ... s...sweet land of liberty." Holding his head back again, I unfastened the golden buttons on his dress uniform and opened it. "Of thee, I sing. Land where my f...f....fathers died." I climbed up off his lap as I pulled the knife from my belt. "Land of the pilgrim's p...pride." I felt down his rib cage to find the last one. "From every mountainside." I thrust the blade hard up under his rib and straight into his heart, just as I had been trained. "Let f...f...freedom ring." As I did, I folded his jacket over my hand to stop blood from seeping over my uniform.

His eyes widened as he stared at me and tried to speak. "Night night, Randall," I said again, in my best motherly voice as I let go of the knife and raised a blood-coated finger to my lips and tasted it. "D...don't try to say anything. Just go to sleep." He blinked, a tear running down his cheek, and he slumped limply against the side of the cubicle. I calmly felt for the pulse in his neck, and as soon as I was sure he was dead, I stepped back. I didn't remove the knife, which certainly would have gotten more blood on me.

I pulled out my hanky and wiped the handle down. Sure, they would find my DNA on him – there was no doubt about that – but there were so many exercises that we'd been performing over the last eleven weeks, where any of us could've come into physical contact with him. Yep, there would be my DNA...and the DNA of twenty others. Even the knife couldn't be traced back to me as I had stolen it. I did feel a pang of guilt for leaving him to be found in

21

such an undignified position, but I'm a bit of a softy about that sort of thing.

I stepped out of the cubicle and washed my hands and face. Once more, humming 'My Country Tis of Thee,' I went back into the main barrack room, carefully checking it to see if the bathroom visitor had left or not. I was extremely fortunate that the room was empty.

I walked to my bunk, picked up the book and placed it back into the bedside cabinet so that there was no direct evidence that I had been in the barracks, and I climbed out of the back window that faced away from the compound.

I then spent the rest of the morning ensuring I was seen around the parade ground by as many men, women, officers, and instructors as possible.

It took about an hour before he was discovered, and of course, the base was immediately locked down.

In the following days, I was subjected to boring interviews with military police, as was everyone. I was on the suspect list after the animosity between us was reported. But no-one who had trained with us honestly believed that the shy girl from Arizona had the temperament to retaliate in such a manner against one of our own. Well, that and the fact that they simply didn't have the evidence to charge me. It did, however, have the annoying effect of delaying us from being able to depart by another week.

CHAPTER THREE

GOODBYE SEDONA

They eventually allowed us to leave for a ten-day furlough before receiving our posts. This time I took the fifteen-minute flight home. I'd sent a text to my parents to tell them I was on my way, but they never replied, so I didn't expect anyone to pick me up from the airport.

I come from a very military family, with Papa and most of my aunts and uncles having served. However, I was an embarrassment to Papa as they had all been commissioned officers, and I didn't make the grade for that. Papa was a strict disciplinarian and quick with the back of his hand or belt. While the bible says to honor thy parents, he solely tested that rule with my brother and me. I had pondered not going home, even as late as when I was in a cab taking me up into the mountains. But I did want to see Sedona one last time before being shipped out.

I received details of my first posting before I left. They were going to put me on the U.S.S. Lewis Puller, and I looked it up on the internet to find out it was named after the most decorated man in the Marine Corps. I couldn't find any details about the ship itself, so I was disappointed that it was apparently unimportant. It was also the first time I had heard *her* name. Although in its more proper form of Jennacia Plularian. You know her now as Admiral Jenna Plural of the Solar Confederation. She was just a lieutenant back then and was to be my commanding officer. The post was to be for two years, and although it didn't say it, that clearly meant I was going off-world.

The car pulled up outside my house. I climbed out and grabbed my kit bag from the trunk, walked up the pathway and opened the door, which my parents rarely locked, despite my objections. I went inside. My brother grunted at me from the couch where he was playing video games. I dropped my kit bag in the hallway and went to the kitchen, where my mother was cooking.

"Oh, hi honey, did you have a nice time at boot camp?" she asked casually, glancing over her shoulder.

"Hi, m...m...Mama. You make it sound like I just got back from a ch...ch...church summer c...c...camp," I said snappily.

She just sighed and turned back to her counter. "Your father's coming home early tonight. I really must get on with this."

I sighed too and rolled my eyes before heading up to my room. Picking up Mr. Hupperty, my stuffed pink hippopotamus, I curled up on the bed, hugged him tightly to my chest, and went to sleep.

******

"The U.S.S. Lewis Puller?" Papa said with obvious contempt. "I've never even heard of the U.S.S. Lewis Puller. Who is Lewis Puller anyway?"

We were seated at the breakfast table. Papa, a retired naval veteran, had only just asked about my assignment, despite my having been home for ten days. He was not at all impressed, and he made it very clear.

I sat there, somewhat irritated. This was to be my first posting, and he was ruining it. "Lewis Puller was a m...m...Marine who was awarded more m...m...medals than anyone else in America."

"How do you know that?" He scoffed.

"I looked it up."

"Exactly! You don't name ships after people no one's heard of unless they're useless. You should be on that new U.S.S. Constitution."

"She's probably a garbage hauler." That was my kid brother Scott, who sat opposite me. He was a mouthy little shit, still in high school.

"Finish your breakfast, Scotty," my mother called over from the kitchen counter. "The school bus is going to be here in ten minutes."

"Yeah yeah, I'm doing it," he muttered, looking down at his food.

I grinned at him patronizingly and felt a sharp kick under the table. I reciprocated with my Marine-issue boot, causing him to jump up, spilling the milk from his bowl. I had steel toecaps on, nice shiny new ones that went with my new uniform. "Fuck you, you bitch!" He shouted at me.

Papa turned red with rage and stood up. "Watch that mouth of yours, boy! I won't tolerate that language in this house. Apologize to your sister at once."

"She's in the United States Marines, Dad," Scott said incredulously. "Do you think they're gonna talk like powder puffs?"

Papa moved so fast that I barely saw it, and he backhanded Scott violently. My brother staggered, but before my father could strike him again, I was up out of my seat and grabbed his wrist. He glared at me, his face reddening and the vein on his forehead throbbing.

"Is this really how you want my last morning here to be?" I shouted. "I am going out into s...s...space today and I won't be coming back for at least two years. Can we, f...f...for once, f...f...finish something without this d...drama?"

Before he could reply, Scotty snatched up his bag and looked at me sadly. "Have a good war, sis." He strode out as I still held onto Papa's wrist, and the last I saw of him was the back of the door as he slammed it closed behind him. My eyes turned to my father, and I let go of his arm. He instantly moved to slap me around the face, but the Marines don't train you to let that slide. My arm swiftly blocked the strike. My mother moved between us.

"You are an ungrateful brat, Emma Dodgson," Papa said.

"Maybe so, Papa, maybe so." I looked at my mama. "I'm sorry about this."

My mother, afraid of him for most of her life, didn't even make eye contact with me. "Perhaps you should just go," she said.

I fought back the tears in my eyes, not knowing if they were out of sadness or anger. I turned from the table, picked up my kit bag, and headed out the front door. It was to be the last time I ever spoke to my parents. Papa was an angry man, and he had always taken it out with his fists on the rest of us. I kind of both love him and hate him at the same time. He never accepted that I was enlisted and not an officer like him. Hell, my school grades barely qualified me to be enlisted, and no-one would ever consider me for an officer's commission. At least, that's what I thought back then.

That was before Jenna Plural.

There was a cool breeze as I stepped out onto the streets of Sedona for the last time. I loved this old town, up in the mountains of Arizona. I had attended the Sedona Red Rock High School, Home of the Scorpions, and had never really left the tourist town other than trips into Phoenix. I hope to go back there one day, but I digress...

I walked down the street and turned the corner, and I looked out over the valley at the rust-covered mountains with a sigh. I dropped my kitbag and stayed out there for about fifteen minutes staring at the scenery, and then I tapped my watch.

"This is P...Private Emma Dodgson 1313978 to Phoenix base requesting p...p...pick up."

There was a few seconds pause before a voice came back. "We read you Private Dodgson 1313978. You're early. We're not scheduled to pick you up for another two hours."

"Yes, Sir. However, I'm ready, but I can k...kill time if that helps?" I replied.

"It would. I can't get anything out to you for at least an hour."

"Affirmative, Sir. Do you wish to give me a location for p...pick up?"

"Activate your locator, Private. The transport will find you," he advised me.

"Thank you, Sir."

"No problem, Private, and good luck on the Lewis Puller."

I tapped the watch again to disconnect the communications, and then I voice-activated my locator, which sent out a GPS signal that only the US military could pick up. I picked up my bag again and walked into town, stopping at a small café. It wasn't very busy, and I ordered a coffee and a cooked breakfast.

As I ate, I got lost in my thoughts, and I didn't see Calvin Butler come in. "Hey, Em."

I looked up at my old high school boyfriend and half-smiled. This was awkward. I had only recently broken up with him because I was leaving. He was headed to university on a football scholarship, and our lives were on very different paths. "Hey, C...C...Cal."

He slipped into the seat opposite me, and as I looked at those big brown eyes, I felt my heart beating fast. The guy was such a honey. "I went to your house, and your parents said you'd already left. I just wanted to say goodbye."

"How did you n...n....know I was here?"

"I didn't. I work in the hardware store next door, remember? I saw you as I was headed into work." He sat back.

"I'm sorry things didn't w...w...work out between us," I said, feeling a little uncomfortable at this unexpected and uninvited reunion. It'd been so hard telling him we were over and watching his heart break into pieces.

Cal shrugged. "They still can. I care about you, and I know you still care about me."

I sighed wearily, not wanting to do this all over again. "We have d...different lives now. You're going off to college, then become some c...c...corporate financier, and I'll be fighting P...P...Peons around the rings of Saturn."

Cal sighed. "You wanna fight? That's fine, but why not do it here? You know the war is headed this way. Texas has already fallen, and there's fighting already going on east of here. You don't need to leave."

"Even if I didn't have to leave, it's all d...d...done and dusted now. It's not like I could tell the US Marine C...Corps, 'Hey, I wanna stay at h...home.' They tell me where to g...go, when to eat, and when to s...sleep."

Calvin gave a sigh of resignation, but he didn't give up. "I saw a future for us. We get married, get a little house and a couple of kids. Boys who grow up to be little jocks," he smiled, but I didn't return it.

"Hey, I didn't get a sc...sc...scholarship and the grades for c...c... college. Military service was always going to be c...compulsory for me."

"Yeah, but military service is just for two years. You signed up to the Marines as a non-conscript regular. The minimum requirement is six years."

"As a c...conscript, I'd be army infantry, virtually cannon fodder. At least this w...way, I'll have some sort of c...career out of it."

"That's more important than us?"

"Cal," I said sharply. "Stop trying to m...make this even harder. You know my s...situation at home. I always told you that I would g...get out at the first opportunity. Anyway, I'm p...proud to be a M...M...Marine, and I'm going to make a c...career of it. You're going to find a n...nice girl and settle down in your h...house with your two boys." Before he could say any more, my communicator buzzed. "Private Dodgson, go ahead." My eyes were still on Calvin but quickly dropped to my wrist communicator as I heard an Australian woman singing. "Pack up your troubles in your old kit bag and smile, smile, smile."

"Excuse me?" I said into the device.

"G'day, Private Dobson, this is Stacey Airlines. I'll be your pilot for your one-way trip to hell."

I looked up at Calvin with wide eyes, and he looked as confused as me. "Excuse me, ma'am, can you c...clarify that?" I asked.

"I'm your ride to Manassas, you moron," the voice came back. "Lieutenant Stacey Grant of the United States Navy. I'm about to put down at your location."

"Ma'am, this is a down t....town high street. You really can't land a sh...shuttle here. Let me know where I can m...move to, and I will m...m...meet you there."

"Something wrong with your voice, mate, or is it some weird arse interference?"

"It's m...m...my voice."

There was a pause before she came back, sounding genuinely apologetic. "Aww, no shit, mate! Sorry. Anyway, this ain't no shuttle, Private. I'm in a Python Interceptor."

"They sent a fighter to p...pick me up, m...ma'am?"

"Don't you watch the news, Dobson? Arizona is a designated war zone. You have Peons less than fifty miles from this location. Uncle Sam doesn't want his nice, new recruit to start her career as a big mass of bullet-ridden jelly."

It was only then that I could hear the roar of the engines. Dust started to blow up from the road covering the surrounding parked cars, and everybody started to come out of the shop doorways down the street. Then the sleek black craft descended out of the clouds and landed slap bang in the middle of the road. Calvin looked at it and then back at me.

"I guess that's m...my ride," I said to him softly.

He came out with me, carrying my kit bag, and I felt the eyes of the entire street upon me. The cockpit of the Python Interceptor opened up, and the pilot looked down at me as the engines died. "G'day mate. Private Emma Dobson?"

I gave her a sharp salute, and she half-heartedly returned it. "It's D...Dodgson, Ma'am."

"What?"

"My name. It's Dodgson, not Dobson."

Grant shrugged, "Yeah, well, unless you need to give your boyfriend a blowjob to keep him sweet, we gotta get moving."

I flushed bright pink, and any chance of a romantic goodbye with Calvin was gone.

I grabbed my kit bag from him and simply said, "I'll s...see you around sometime." Then I climbed onto the wing, stowed my bag behind the empty seat, and climbed into it. As the canopy closed, I looked down at Calvin, but he was already walking away. I placed the headphones on to hear the pilot and sat back in the seat, fastening my seat belt.

The pilot called Control to radio in her flight plan. We certainly didn't want to be shot down as an enemy aircraft. "This is Lieutenant Stacey Grant lifting off from Sedona. Transmitting navigation routes. I'll be flying around the front lines. ETA in Manassas, in just over twelve minutes."

"That's a copy, Lieutenant Grant. Clear skies to you," came the flight control reply. I looked once more for Calvin, and saw him standing on the corner of the street where he'd turned around to watch. I gave him a wave, but he didn't reciprocate, so I let my hand fall onto my lap and looked away as the craft rose vertically up into the sky.

I decided this pilot was a little bit crazy as she pulled up before the DE compensators came online, and I was pushed violently back into my seat.

Everything became virtually a blur to me. I could barely understand how this Stacey Grant could even follow what was happening. However, I didn't have time to think about it. Within seconds, Grant threw the craft into a roll. "Shit, those motherfuckers pushed forward the frontline further than we thought." To be in the company of Stacey Grant, one had to get used to her rather salty language. "We've got three Dutch Viper class fighters coming up after us."

"C....can we lose them, ma'am?"

"Lose them?" Lieutenant Grant laughed. "No, Private Dobson, we blow those fuckers out of the sky."

"If you say so, ma'am," I said nervously.

"Hey, trust me, I'm Australian." She giggled like a twelve-year-old schoolgirl as we suddenly flipped down and began to spiral.

I looked out of the canopy windows and felt momentary nausea as the world spun around me. She then straightened and shot straight back up into the air. I was startled to see an enemy aircraft appear to drop down in front of us. We were mere feet away from it as Grant fired the primary weapons. There was a hiss, and then a bang as the rear of the enemy aircraft erupted into flame and began to spin out of control, plummeting to the Earth. "That's one of the tulip fuckers." The foul-mouthed Aussie punched the roof of the canopy in celebration. We again fell into a spin as I saw her evade a couple of missiles on our left. "I hope you haven't pissed your pants back there, Private." She laughed.

"I am doing quite fine, ma'am," I said, just as Grant spun us in a one-eighty turn and fired straight into the front of another craft. We shook slightly as shrapnel from the exploding vessel hit us, but this pilot was darn good. The final pilot started working out her tactics and got on our tail, and he or she didn't move from that position. Our craft bumped up and down in random directions as missile after missile came at our rear. Grant's sudden silence made me uneasy as I realized we were in trouble. Then suddenly, she pushed her craft into a dive and headed straight to the ground at an unbelievable speed. The darn Peon on our tail stayed on us, copying the dive and still firing. Stacey pulled up sharply at what seemed like inches from the ground, and the engines whined in protest. If she had intended for him to hit the ground before pulling up, she failed, and he stuck with us. However, as he pulled up, she released a ton of flack straight down onto his canopy. I didn't see what happened, but I heard the craft explode as we shot off across the US and out of the contested airspace.

CHAPTER FOUR

ABOARD THE CHESTY

W e landed just outside the cosmodrome in a small field of other Interceptors. Grant waited until I climbed out and followed me as naval personnel rushed around doing post-flight checks.

"Welcome home, ma'am." A young, heavily built Marine sergeant walked up to us with a beaming smile, but the smile was not to last long.

"Wow," Stacey said somewhat irritably. "I must be way off course then."

"Ma'am?" the sergeant frowned.

"This must be Wagga."

"I'm not sure I understand, ma'am."

"You said welcome home. My home's in Australia, mate."

"Yes, ma'am, no offense intended, ma'am."

"None was taken, Sergeant Hardy. Carry on." She stepped past him and headed off toward the astrodome. Hardy muttered something about her being a bitch and turned his wrath upon me. "What are you staring at, Private?"

"Nothing, Sir." I stood at attention, immediately realizing my mistake, but it was too late.

"Get your lazy ass over there." He indicated where another group of privates stood nervously near the entrance of the cosmodrome, and I saw Grant giving them a cheery wave as she passed them. I put my kit over my shoulder and started to walk over to them, but Hardy shouted, "Double time, Private Dobson!" Annoyed at my name once more being incorrect, I broke into a run and reached the group thirty seconds later. There were five of them. I don't remember their names, but the one that can't go without mentioning was Kelsey Anthony. She was the closest thing I had to a friend in those first days. Sadly, it was not to last as she, too, would ultimately become a problem for me. She smiled at me as I approached, being the only other female in the group.

"Thank God there's another woman around!" These were her first words to me. "This testosterone around me was getting somewhat tiresome."

One of the men grinned at us. "You should enjoy the opportunity, Anthony. I hear there aren't many men on this ship." I think his name was Berkeley, but I am not sure. Let's just go with Berkeley.

"Fuck you, Berkeley. Not even if you were the last man on Earth."

He puffed up his chest in a vain effort to look sexy. "Well, that's fine because we're not gonna be on Earth in a few hours, and I'll be all yours, baby."

"And that gets you two hundred push-ups, Marine!" Hardy said, coming up behind us. Berkeley looked like he was going to argue. "Four hundred. Hit the dirt, mister."

Berkley complied, and I smiled at the sergeant, but not for long. "If you don't want to join him, Dobson, take that stupid grin off your face." Turning back to Berkeley, he said, "if I catch you sexually harassing female troopers again, you will spend the rest of this voyage in the M.E.T. without pay and face a court-martial on your return." No one spoke; the only sound was the huffing and puffing of Berkeley as he did his push-ups. Hardy turned around to each Marine in turn. "Is this the best they can give me? I guess that's what happens when you're on a shit stain of a ship." Hardy sighed with resignation. "Well, don't just stand there. Get moving, at the double!" We broke into a run and went through the astrodome's large rusty doors and into the wreck of a base.

It was just as Mr. Phelkar described in his book. Dilapidated, with signs of bomb damage. The U.S.S. Lewis Puller was just like he said as well. A heaving wreck of a vessel that was badly patched.

"Everybody halt!" Hardy ordered. We all complied and stood at attention. "Everyone line up in front of the cargo bay ramp."

Again, we complied, with the five of us facing out from the clapped-out old vessel. We stood in an at-ease position. Hardy was about to speak, but then appeared to notice something behind us.

"Attention!" he shouted. "Officer on the deck!"

At first, I was confused, as some incredibly hot co-ed in an officer's uniform stepped out in front of us. She bore lieutenant chevrons and was undoubtedly one of the most beautiful women I had ever seen. She had long, light brown hair tied very neatly into a ponytail, and blue eyes that seemed to sparkle. I took an instant dislike to this woman who looked like she was a cheerleader, and not a badass Marine.

"The new recruits, ma'am," Hardy informed her.

"Good morning, boys and girls. My name is Jenna Plural, and I'm the Second Officer onboard the U.S.S. Lewis Puller. I know you're probably itching to get your hands on the enemy, but unfortunately, it won't be on this trip. Your duties will be in support. And I regret to inform you that, for most of this mission, you will be uploaded in the M.E.T. for most of the voyage. You will only be downloaded if we are attacked en route to our destination or other unforeseen circumstances arise. When we're ready to launch, you'll be uploaded, and most likely not downloaded again until we return to Earth. I apologize that you won't get much experience on this voyage, but you will get full credit for your service. Until you're uploaded, you can use the crew cabins, as your more experienced crewmates are already uploaded. However, you'll have pre-launch ship preparation duties that Sergeant Hardy will hand out to you. You have one hour to get yourself ready and stow your kit. Dismissed." She turned away and spoke to Hardy.

Kelsey turned to me. "Come on, let's go find a cabin before the guys take the best ones."

I grinned and followed her inside, eager to find a cabin where I could shower and change. We grabbed the first one we saw. It was a four-man berth, but we had it to ourselves. There was no gender segregation in the military, but I was happy not to share with men. "So, where are you from?"

I told her as I unpacked my kit bag and asked her in return. "I'm from Chicago and grew up there. This is my first time away from home for basic training," she told me.

"S...same here. My father was m...military, but we never moved with him."

We both took turns showering, and I put on a fresh uniform, and together we both reported for duty.

As you already know, the U.S.S. Lewis Puller, affectionately known as The Chesty, was a small, dark, dreary ship. As Kelsey and I explored, our excitement turned to grim depression. This was to be our home for two years, and its only redeeming quality was that we'd spend most of it in the nothingness of the M.E.T.

We met a woman dressed in civvies when we got down to the engine area. She wore immodestly tight jeans over an equally tight hoodie and spoke with a thick New York accent. She smiled as she came up to us. "Hey, nice to see some fresh faces." I was unsure how to address her at first, for she bore no indication of her rank, so I left it to Kelsey to say, "nice to meet you, ma'am."

The redheaded woman grinned. "I'm not a ma'am. But obviously, you can't tell that while I'm off duty. Gunnery Sergeant Helen Tracker. I'm chief tech of this vintage pride of the fleet."

Kelsey chuckled. "Vintage? Nice way to put it, sergeant."

Helen returned the grin. "Well, don't let Lieutenant Plural hear you diss the U.S.S. Lewis Puller. She'll put you on report."

"She likes this ship?" I asked wide-eyed.

"Oh, she knows it's a heap of junk like the rest of us." Tracker laughed. "But she believes you should take pride in any ship you serve aboard. This ship should have been retired many years ago. However, since we lost our last construction base on Mars, we gotta make do and mend."

"We're losing this war, aren't we?" Kelsey said, much to my horror.

"D...don't ever say that," I said curtly. I really hated defeatists. "America hasn't lost a war in hundreds of years, and it's not about to now. It's outrageous to even suggest such an outcome." There was silence as both Tracker and Kelsey stared at me and my rising anger.

"Umm, yes, well, there is a welcome party in the mess," Helen said. "Come by in about thirty minutes, and we'll have a proper Marine welcome for you."

I said nothing, for my blood was still boiling, but Kelsey smiled and said, "Now that sounds like a plan."

Tracker smiled at her, glanced awkwardly at me, and walked off. We continued our tour of the ship, familiarizing ourselves with its layout and emergency procedures until it was time to go to the mess. It was small and cramped like most of the ship, and about a half dozen Marines and a couple of naval personnel were already knocking back cold beers. It was a mixture of new and a couple of veteran crewmen, and Berkeley was there trying to hit on some woman who was obviously uninterested. The guy was a creep, and there was no mistaking that. It was a long time since the military tolerated such acts, but it still didn't stop them from happening. Sexual impropriety was your one-way ticket out of the military and into prison. I could see that Berkeley was in for a short career. I pondered dealing with him myself, but he was dead three weeks later anyway.

A Lance Corporal, who I later found out was called Neuman, was frying up eggs, bacon, and sausages. When the Marines scoffed them down, he protested. "You have to save some for the officers."

"You can make them some ham sandwiches," laughed another Marine.

Someone threw us both cans of Budweiser, which we cracked open.

"Hey guys," Helen Tracker stepped into the room, grinning. "It plays merry hell with your system if you go through the M.E.T. intoxicated." She'd changed into the Marine uniform but wore a pink hoodie over it. I couldn't help but think how inappropriate that was.

Now, I know what you're thinking. That I was some kind of prudish stuck-up little know-it-all who played by the book. But you'd be wrong. I just think a certain level of dignity should be maintained in the Corps.

The casual laid back atmosphere was really fun, and I couldn't help but warm to these guys. A pleasant time was had by most, until the sergeant came in and brought it to an end.

Hardy was his usual unpleasant self, but he put Berkeley on bathroom duties which pleased both Kelsey and me, so we didn't really complain when he had us inventorying the cargo supplies in the hold. It was a laborious mind-numbing task. However, we were interrupted when Lieutenant Plural, in a rather indecently small tank top and shorts, came running down the deck with Stacey Grant close behind her.

"Their shuttle has just disappeared off the radar." Lieutenant Plural was telling the young Australian. "It must have come down somewhere near Virginia Beach."

"I could take out an Interceptor. It'll be much faster." Grant suggested.

"Too fast. If they bailed out, you'd hardly spot an individual."

"Good point, boss. We can send up a drone. It can fly in low and has a fairly good range before it needs refueling." As they passed us, we stood to attention and saluted. Lieutenant Plural gave a brief, half-hearted salute back, and oh so unprofessionally, Grant gave me a wink.

"Go for it, and while you're doing that, I'll see if I can get satellite coverage of the area," Lieutenant Plural said as the two went on to the main hub of the base.

Kelsey and I looked at each other, wondering what was going on, but we just continued with our work. Fifteen minutes later, we saw a drone going up into the air from the other side of the astrodome's wall. We listened to the hum of the engine until it disappeared from our view and then simply carried on checking off the boxes. About thirty minutes later, Lieutenant Plural came running out of the hub. She headed over to where cars were parked on the outer circle of the astrodome and jumped into one. Seconds later, she tore out of the base.

When we were finishing up, the car with Mr. Phelkar and Lieutenant Plural pulled back into the astrodome. We both watched as he got out. He was staring at the Lewis Puller, looking horrified at the vessel.

"Well, isn't he a cutie," Kelsey said with a grin. "I'd love to wrap my legs around that face."

"Plus, he has that adorable English accent that you young American girls love so much." I turned to see Grant grinning at us.

Kelsey flushed pink and stood to attention. "Yes, ma'am."

"What about you, Dobson? Wouldn't you like a piece of that arse?"

It was my turn to flush, and I just blustered incoherently, which caused Grant to grin. "At ease, ladies. Don't bust a blood vessel, Dobson."

"It's D...D...Dodgson, ma'am."

"Yeah yeah, whatever," she muttered but was already stepping past us and walking up to Mr. Phelkar. "She ain't as bad as she looks," she said to him.

He turned to face her. "Lieutenant Grant, I presume?" he said, as Lieutenant Plural turned toward me and beckoned me over.

"Got it in one, mate," Grant was saying.

Lieutenant Plural handed me his bag and said, "Stow it aboard the ship." She then sent Kelsey to drive the car away, as I headed up the ramp, back into the ship.

That shithead Hardy was waiting for me in the doorway. "Have you finished that inventory?"

"Yes, Sergeant. The lieutenant asked me to put away this bag for the civilian visitor."

"Then move yourself, Dobson! And get to the M.E.T. It's time for upload."

I sighed. Would anyone ever get my name right? Hardy looked down the ramp to where Mr. Phelkar and Lieutenant Grant were coming up. He said nothing more to me, so I hurried past, wondering where the hell I was to put this bag and wondering why it was so freaking dirty. Ultimately, I just stored it in my cabin, which I guess was as good a place as any. I then headed over to get uploaded.

I'd only been in an M.E.T. once before. They gave us the experience back in basic training, so it wouldn't come as a surprise to us. The one thing I would always be uncomfortable with was removing our clothes, storing them in cabin lockers, and then heading down the corridor to the M.E.T. room. But that was life in the modern USMC. We double-timed it to get there before any of the guys did. And fortunately, we made it. I went in first. I met Helen Tracker, and there were no preliminaries. Tracker barked the orders. "Stand in the circle." I complied. "Raise your arms." I complied again, and there was a flash of light this time. As the glow faded, I looked back at Tracker, wondering just for a moment if it had gone wrong. "We're under attack! Move out and get kitted up!" She instructed. Not until much later did I realize that three weeks had passed, and we were only halfway to our Mars destination.

Chapter Five

Boarded

I headed out into the corridor. Two other Marines had come out ahead of me, and already another was appearing behind me. "Faster, Dobson! You're not walking down the aisle at your wedding!" Sergeant Hardy barked.

I followed the others to the port-side corridor and found a uniform waiting for me on the floor with chest armor and a snap pistol. I dressed quickly, as I was trained to. Kelsey came to my side, looking much more nervous than I felt. We helped fasten each other's armor, and there was a buzz of conversation as we all tried to work out what was going on.

It fell silent when Lieutenant Plural stood at the end of the corridor. We came to attention. She waited until all fell silent, standing with legs apart and hands behind her back. We felt the tension grow, and the only sound was the soft hum of the engine.

She swung out a fist and hit the intercom. "Froggy comes a-calling!" She paused. "They want to take your ship!" She paused again. "But just like the man this ship is named after; we shall give them no quarter." Another pause. "We shall make them pay in Peon blood for every square foot of our ship!" Her voice rose as she spoke. "They're coming from the port side, and we'll expect full hull penetration. We will not let these Peon bastards win the day." Then she screamed out, "We are United States Marines! What are we?"

"United States Marines!" We replied in unison, and it echoed around the ship.

"Fall in on the port corridor and prepare for battle." She raised her fist and pumped in the air three times, chanting, "U.S.A.! U.S.A.! U.S.A.!" In unison, we stamped our right foot on the floor in the unofficial salute of our commanding officer. Then, we ran to our positions and turned to face the wall with weapons raised to our hips.

An eerie silence fell all around us, and only the slight hum of the engines and vibrations of the decks could be heard.

We waited.

There was a boom, and it rang through the deck in an aftershock. The line of Marines tensed.

"Easy boys and girls! It's gonna be just like squishing frog spawn!" Lieutenant Plural called down the line. "Pascal, stop scratching your ass! And Butterwick, hold up that ugly head of yours! You're killing Peons, not going down on your boyfriend." The others laughed at this. I didn't get what it meant.

I felt very tense as the drilling started. I knew what was coming. We'd undergone intensive and repetitive training on repelling boarders, but that didn't prepare you for that feeling in your gut, knowing that, in a few moments, it was kill or be killed. Next to us, the bulkhead suddenly disintegrated before our eyes, and the two Marines in front of it fired into the dark. I saw the body of a man in the light blue uniform of the French fall through the hole, and suddenly, the Marine next to me flew back against the wall, his face a bloodied pulp.

When the hole opened up in front of me, I was face to face with a large angry looking woman, and I fired. As she went down, I felt the thrill coursing through my veins at my first killing of a Peon, and I found myself laughing as I continued to fire at the scum.

I saw Kelsey go down in my peripheral vision, but I could do nothing but hold the line. Then I heard Lieutenant Plural cry out, "Grenade!"

Hastily I stumbled away from the hole and over the bodies of comrades and Peons, following my teammates out of the corridor and away from the expected explosion. It turned out to just be a pesky flashbang. When we reached the larger hallway, a couple of us turned back and fired down the corridor. Berkeley suddenly went down by my side, with a hole in his head just above his right eye. I was convinced I would die that day, but I was going to make sure I took out as many of those damn Peons as I could.

Like a swarming mass, the Peons came on, and we turned in full retreat.

Hardy and I stopped and turned back to fire again, but my weapon clicked. I realized I hadn't followed ammunition protocol. As I ducked behind a doorway, I pulled another clip from my belt and reloaded the weapon. When

I looked up, I saw Hardy looking at me, shaking his head dismissively. *Damn it to hell*, I thought. I'd fouled up in front of the Sergeant.

There was no time to discuss the issue, as once more, we fired. I lost track of how many I killed, but it was clear, there was no way we were going to win. We fell back further, fighting all the way as our comrades fell one by one, until it was only myself and Hardy left in that area of the ship. That's when the miracle happened. I had been praying for one, and God answered my call. The Peons started to fall back. I looked at Hardy, but he was as confused as me.

"What's going on, Sergeant?" I asked uneasily, but he shook his head and shrugged.

"I don't know, Dobson." He edged forward as the last of the Peons disappeared down the corridor.

The intercom came on, and the captain's voice could be heard. "Lieutenant Plural, stand down. Purple sky, I repeat, purple sky. Stand down."

"What does he mean by 'purple sky,' Sarge?" I asked, but Hardy just shook his head again, not knowing the answer. While reading Mr. Phelkar's account, I found out that it meant that it was a genuine order and not something said under duress.

Only then did I notice that Hardy had a bloody wound on his shoulder as, once more, the intercom crackled into life. "Lieutenant Plural, confirm that you have stood down? Report to the cockpit."

"Stand down, confirmed." We heard her reply aggressively.

We met up with the other surviving Marines, just as Lieutenant Plural came into the area, "Get Tracker to download Doctor Archer and see to the wounded. Then start racking and stacking our dead in the cargo hold."

"What about the Peon's dead and wounded?" A Marine asked.

"Stick them out the airlock," she barked, heading away from him.

"The wounded, Ma'am?" He inappropriately questioned.

"I don't like repeating myself, Reeves," she said, not looking back. "They don't take prisoners in space, so neither do we."

We started to see to our own wounded, but there was a stunned silence when the captain's message that the United States had surrendered and that the war was officially over came over the comms. We just stood there in disbelief. "Sarge, come on. You n...need to get that seen to," I said, at last, referring to his wound.

"It's fine." He stared at me, and I shrugged it off. If he wanted to bleed out, that was his affair. It was only then that everything started to sink in as I looked around at the carnage throughout the ship.

As Hardy took over the organization of the dead, I slipped away to check on Kelsey. I headed back to the corridor where it all began. I found her sitting with her back and head against the wall, very much alive. "Hey," I said as I approached her. She opened her eyes and looked up at me with a start.

"Hey, Dodgson." She said weakly.

I looked her up and down with a frown. I couldn't see anywhere on her that she could have been injured. "Where did they get you?"

She pointed up to her left shoulder. "Right here."

I crouched down beside her and took a look. Indeed, there was a bullet hole in the edge of her uniform, but the projectile had barely grazed her. I had injured myself more seriously with a paper cut. I looked at her with incredible disdain. "This is barely a scratch."

"It hurts like fuck," she snapped at me.

"Then we best get you to the med bay, hadn't we?" I said curtly.

As I started to help Kelsey up, I heard a moan nearby. I left her and told her to wait while I checked on this other survivor.

I looked down at a Peon, trying to rise up. He was clutching a gut wound, and as he managed to turn himself over, he looked up at me, and his eyes widened in terror. I looked down at the scum with contempt. We had officially surrendered, but could I just walk away or, even worse, help him? I unfastened my holster and slipped out my snap pistol.

"Pardon me, Monsieur." I couldn't speak French, but I knew a few words. With him crying, "Non, non, non!", I let off a round right into his face. He slumped back. Behind me, Kelsey gasped. I looked back at her and shook my head in disbelief. "Come on, get up," I said, pulling up her arm.

As she got to her feet, she looked at me, terrified. "What are you going to say about me?"

I shrugged. "Nothing. I'm not an officer, nor an NCO. It's none of my business."

Oh, but I so wanted to make it my business. I felt nothing but contempt for her.

We made our way to the medical center. Doctor Archer, whose name I didn't know until long after she'd died, looked up at us as we entered. She was surrounded by wounded, with every bunk in use and some on the floor. "Unless you're dying, you're going to have to wait outside."

"I'm unharmed," I said. "It's my colleague here that requires assistance. "

"Well, she can wait outside, and you can help me. They didn't download my nurses."

I slipped off my jacket, and for the next twenty minutes, I helped clean up wounds and applied bandages, while the doctor attended to the more serious cases. I then tagged the ones who'd died while receiving treatment. During that time, I was trying to get my head around the idea the United States had surrendered. It wasn't possible. The captain had got it wrong.

I was distracted from my dark thoughts by a scuffling outside, and I heard Kelsey cry out, and someone shouted at her in French.

The door burst open, and two men in light blue Peon uniforms and holding handguns stepped into the room, pushing Kelsey ahead of them. A Marine nearby tried to get up from his bunk, and I realized it was Sergeant Hardy, who I would find out, had collapsed from his wounds. One of the Peons pointed his gun toward him, and he

51

lay back down. They barked orders at us, but none of us could understand the words, and as they walked around the room, checking the dead and wounded for weapons, it was clear we'd been told not to resist.

When one of them came up for me, he looked me up and down with a lewd sneer. He stared at my chest. I'd developed rather ample breasts, which was somewhat of an impairment as a Marine, and frequently drew glances from less eloquent males and some females. He reached down, and for a moment, I thought he was going to touch me inappropriately, but he just removed my snap pistol from its holster. He muttered something at me, and his companion laughed. However, they headed back to the door, with the other Peon turning back to say something and, with his hands, indicated we were to stay in this room. I stood staring at the door, fuming in anger.

"Come on, Private. We still have work to do," Doctor Archer said to me, and we continued working with the injured.

It was almost an hour later when, to my surprise, Lieutenant Plural and Mr. Phelkar came in under armed guard.

"I need more help. Tell these idiots that I need my team downloaded!" The doctor demanded.

"They're not going to listen. They're going to have you upload any wounded," Lieutenant Plural replied disinterestedly.

"Half of these men have shrapnel with them! They can't be uploaded until I remove it." The doctor vehemently protested.

"Do the best you can, Doctor," Lieutenant Plural sounded frustrated. "However, first, I need you to take a bullet out of my stomach."

"Sorry, Lieutenant, you're still walking. You'll have to wait your turn. I have other priorities of a more serious nature."

"I really must insist, doctor. You *need* to remove a bullet, and you need to do it behind *that* curtain there." She indicated to the privacy screen of a small examination cubicle.

The doctor was about to object, but realized Lieutenant Plural was up to something.

"Come on then, Lieutenant."

She led Lieutenant Plural behind a screen, and the guard made to follow, but Mr. Phelkar stopped him and said something in French. The guard looked annoyed, but turned and headed out. I was unable to hear what was going on behind the curtain, but the doctor looked mad as she stepped out from the cubicle and headed off to where she stored her meds.

A female Peon officer entered and, after looking around, she headed over to Mr. Phelkar.

She spouted French at him, then spat in his face. I made to move toward them, but Kelsey grabbed my arm.

The Peon continued shouting at him in French until the doctor went behind the curtain again, and she followed her in.

It all happened so fast, as Lieutenant Plural stepped out from behind the curtain.

"Hey, you!" She called to one of the guards. "Something is wrong with one of your people here."

The guard stepped over, and as he passed Lieutenant Plural, she shoved an injector into his neck. As he went down, she pulled his pistol from its holster and shot the final guard. He fell back over a bunk where Private Mitchell lay, and he snapped the Peon's neck. A cheer went up from the surviving troopers, and Lieutenant Plural had to tell them, "Shut up!"

The door opened, and two other guards came in. The one in the lead went down from a shot from Lieutenant Plural. Phelkar jumped on the other, and a struggle ensued. He got him on the floor, and Lieutenant Plural brought her boot down onto his head with a twist.

"You're making a habit of saving my life, Mr. Phelkar," Lieutenant Plural smiled at him as she offered him a hand up.

"It seems to be a mutual arrangement, Lieutenant Plural, but you're most welcome," Mr. Phelkar said with a most charming smile.

Lieutenant Plural turned to the Marine who'd been of assistance. "Up for the fight, Private Mitchell?"

He looked delighted but said, "Ma'am, I'd give anything to kill Peons right now, but...." He pulled back the sheet covering his legs and showed us the mangled mess of his knee.

"You always were a shirker, Mitchell," Lieutenant Plural grinned and squeezed his shoulder reassuringly. "Listen to Doctor Archer, and don't grope the nurses."

He laughed. "I'll try not to, Lieutenant, especially as there aren't any."

Lieutenant Plural noticed me. "What is your name, Private?" she asked.

"Dodgson, Ma'am," I told her.

"You don't look injured."

"No, Ma'am, I'm not," I replied, hoping she would take me with her.

"You up for a scrap with the Peons?"

"Yes, Ma'am," I replied eagerly.

"Oh no, you don't," Doctor Archer said to her. "If you can't get me my nurses, you can at least leave Dodgson here to help me."

Lieutenant Plural pondered this, and to my great disappointment, she replied, "Carry on, Dodgson." Turning to the doctor, she said, "You have her for now."

"Give the Peon fuckers hell from us, Lieutenant!" Another Marine called over to her, and she smiled at him and raised a defiant fist, before stepping out the door.

My attitude towards the Lieutenant did an immediate about-turn. She was fighting back! Personally, I'd rather die for America than see America die. Hope was rekindled within me.

I glared at the doctor, who now had her back to me, as she moved over to check on Mitchell. I slowly stepped behind the curtain where Lieutenant Plural had been and looked down where the Peon woman who'd spat into Mr. Phelkar's face lay. I stepped over to her and pulled the curtain closed behind me. The woman on the floor opened her eyes just in time to see me place my foot on her throat. She struggled, fear in her eyes as she tried to breathe, and grabbed futilely at my steel-capped Marine-issue boot as I pushed down harder. Her eyes began to bulge, and a wave of pleasure ran through my body, as I waited a minute after she'd stopped moving to ensure she was dead before removing it. I sighed regretfully at not having the opportunity to take my time and enjoy it more.

CHAPTER SIX

THE JANGLE BERRY

I often hear people say war is hell. Personally, I don't get it. There is simply nothing better than annihilating the enemies of America.

Although I'd technically lost my first battle, the idea that Jenna Plural wouldn't accept the surrender and was fighting back had me pumped up and exhilarated. I felt bitter towards the doctor who'd stopped me from leaving with someone I now thought of as a goddamn heroine. You'll know what I mean if you ever have the privilege of meeting Jenna Plural. That is, of course, if you're a patriot and love America.

As I stepped out from behind that curtain, I took the opportunity to retrieve my snap pistol from the dead Peon who'd had taken it from me, and I returned it to my holster. I continued assisting the annoying doctor for probably about another hour, and spent that time wondering what Jenna Plural was doing. When there was nothing more for me to do, I just stood in a corner and glared at her until she eventually noticed and, condescendingly, said, "If you want to go, Private Dodgson, just go."

I must admit that a grin crossed my face as she said this, but as I turned to Kelsey and asked, "Are you coming?", any joy I felt turned to disgust as she shook her head with a terrified look on her face.

So alone, I headed out into the corridor and made my way forward. My snap pistol was out and at the ready. I had no clue where Lieutenant Plural had gone, and I just hoped I would run into her before I ran into the enemy.

No such luck.

"Arrêt!" Someone shouted as I came around a corner, and by the two rifles pointed at me, I concluded it meant 'halt". The Peons had just been standing in the corridor talking quietly. So quietly that I hadn't heard them. I pondered shooting one of them for a moment, but that would have guaranteed my death from the other.

Slowly I raised my hands with the snap pistol still held. He barked another order in his gibberish language, and it didn't take a genius to realize they meant 'drop the weapon,' but I just stared at him and shrugged like I was an ignorant idiot. With the other keeping his rifle pointed at me, he shouldered his own. His eyes on my weapon, he stepped forward, but just as he reached up for it, a loud *ker-chang* startled all of us.

The ceiling-mounted machine guns started to power up. Fear and panic came over my opponents as they looked around, terrified. But not for long. I bought the snap pistol down, and with two shots, one in each head, I stood there smiling proudly. I instinctively reached up to feel the security pin that would stop the automated weaponry from targeting me, and it was my turn to panic. I'd left my jacket, with the only means of keeping me safe, back in the med center. I turned and started to run, but knew I would not make it.

I almost gave up when a young, scared-looking tech came around the corner. "The Peons were panicking so much they just let me go," she told me excitedly.

I'm not proud of what I did next, but I'm sure you understand that it was necessary. I quickly reached up and pulled the pin from her collar. "What the fuck are you doing?" she said, desperately trying to snatch it back, but I pushed her away hard, and the guns began firing. I turned away and shut out the screams, as I headed back to the med center as if nothing had occurred.

There was silence in the med center. Everyone was trying to work out what'd happened. Archer looked up at me, as I grabbed my jacket and put it back on. "What the hell is going on out there, Private?"

"It would appear that Lieutenant Plural has managed to activate the automated defense systems," I said with pride.

"Oh my God, does that bitch know what she's doing?" Archer looked appalled. "There's an extremely high risk of hull punctures! This ship was never designed for it in the first place. The whole installation of it was a screw-up."

I wanted to respond to that. I wanted to tell her how pathetic she was, worrying about her own life over the potential of victory. However, she was a superior officer. The conventions of rank muted me.

"Better dead than being a Peon prisoner," Mitchell said angrily, and I gave him one of my best smiles.

Everyone began talking nervously about what was going on. We need not have worried. The only living Peon left was that commander, who Lieutenant Plural had locked in the bridge with our captain, who had shown his true colors when he continued to capitulate to the enemy. However, for all intents and purposes, Lieutenant Plural was now in charge of the ship.

Everyone fell silent when the intercom chimed. The confident voice of Lieutenant Jenna Plural came over the line. "Doctor, I need three Marines. What have you got for me?"

Archer looked about and saw Kelsey and me. "I'm willing to release Kelsey, Anthony, and you can now have Dodgson, but that's it," the doctor stated firmly.

"I need one more, doctor. If they can walk and hold a gun, patch them up and send them to me," Lieutenant Plural demanded.

"I'll go." We looked over to see Hardy climbing out of his bunk.

"You still have a bullet in you, Sergeant," Archer argued.

"Slap a patch on it," he sneered. "Plural needs me."

"No, Sergeant, I am not discharging you." The doctor stated firmly.

He stepped up and glared down at her. "Look at this face, doctor." He pointed at himself. "Do you see it?"

"What is your point, Sergeant?" The doctor asked irritably.

"Does it look like this face gives a flying fuck about whether you discharge me or not?" He was very aggressive.

Archer, although not the slightest bit intimidated, sighed and turned back to the intercom. "Sergeant Hardy will join you too. However, I will note that he's discharged himself against my advice."

"Noted, Doctor, thank you," Lieutenant Plural replied, and the intercom went off.

"Consider yourself on report for insubordination, Sergeant," Archer told him.

"Yeah, yeah," he said, flipping her off as he headed to the door. "Fall in Dobson and Anthony," he ordered, not looking back.

Kelsey looked like she was going to refuse, but I gave her an aggressive shove toward the door, and she complied.

I can't pronounce the vulgar French name the enemy ship was called. The closest I can get is the Jangle Berry, and that's what most of us called it. I think only Mr. Phelkar was able to pronounce it anyway. Lieutenant Plural was planning on taking the ship by subterfuge. Apparently, this particular design of vessel had a major flaw, in that if you blew all six of its primary personnel airlocks, it would decompress too fast for the defensive systems to respond. The trick was, to be able to blow them all at the same time. To put it simply, we were to take a spacewalk across to that ship and hope that the Peons didn't see us coming. Stacey Grant, who was supposedly an expert on all types of ships, claimed there were various blind spots we could take advantage of.

We all met up in the cargo bay, and apart from us, there was Jenna Plural – of course – as well as two officers I hadn't met before, Harlow and Sakamoto. I didn't even question when I heard that Jenna Plural had assumed the rank of Major during this incident. I was just so pleased she was doing the right thing and that I was part of it.

It was my first day out, and already I'd participated in repelling boarders, and now I was to participate in an operation to take out a French cruiser. I was rather confused when it turned out that the non-American, Tomiko Sakamoto, a Japanese citizen who was working with Jenna on some kind of exchange program, was going to be taking the lead. Don't get me wrong, I truly value our allies, but it only makes sense that Americans take the lead when working together. Kitted out in my EMU suit with a heavy Extra Vehicular Maneuver pack on my back (the correct name for what Mr. Phelkar called a 'Jet Pack.'), I awaited my orders.

"Listen up, Marines," Sakamoto shouted over the suit comms. "We are going to do this by the numbers. Give me a count off." One by one, the Marines counted themselves off, Major Plural was number three, and I was number five. "Okay, power up your packs." As the large cargo bay doors opened, I fired up the pack and felt my feet leave the ground. We all moved out into the void.

It was my first time making a spacewalk outside of a simulator, and I would have thought I'd be more nervous. But I was quite relaxed as I pushed the jets into the forward position and headed out with the line of Marines. I have to admit, I was kind of hoping that not all the Peons would die in the decompression and that I'd have another opportunity for a firefight.

We continued forward until Sakamoto came online. "Time to break formation and head for the airlock you've been designated." Suddenly Sakamoto's voice urgently came online again. "You're drifting off course, Major. Do we have a problem?"

She didn't reply.

I heard the voice of Mr. Phelkar, who was apparently watching from within the Lewis Puller. "She's fine, Lieutenant Sakamoto. Just give me a minute."

"We don't have a fucking minute!" Sakamoto yelled at him. "Everyone standby to abort."

"Belay that order!" Mr. Phelkar shouted.

"You are out of line, Phelkar!" Sakamoto responded viciously.

"I'm okay," Major Plural stated determinedly as she suddenly came back online.

"Major, you will keep it together," Sakamoto demanded.

"I got this. Phelkar, you still out there?"

"Give me a sec." The line went dead, and I looked over to see Major Plural was back on course. I admit I started to grow nervous as I realized our commander had appeared to have lost it momentarily. I couldn't help but wonder as I realized if that was why Sakamoto had been put in charge. Did she have some issues with doing a space walk? Many people did. No matter how many people are around you, there's a great sense of isolation stepping out into that void.

I turned my attention back to the destination and pushed the thrusters forward, increasing my velocity toward the Peon ship. As the airlock I'd been designated to came into view, I adjusted my course for greater accuracy and started to slow down. The last thing I wanted to do was smack into the hull. My mind went back to my simulator training, and lining myself up, I cut the engines and allowed myself to drift on to it. All I could hear was my breathing, as I pulled the limpet mines from my belt and began to line them up around the door.

Sakamoto voice came over the comms. "Okay, Marines, they will have already detected us, but you have about three minutes before they will be ready to retaliate, so make it count. Give me a count-off when everything is in place."

One by one, the Marines counted off, and Sakamoto said, "Okay, on my countdown, set your charges for one minute. That's all the time we have, ladies and gentlemen. Make it count. Three, two, one, mark!"

I set my charges on Sakamoto's mark and put my suit into reverse thrust. I moved my way back out of range, yet I still felt the blast's shockwave. Fortunately, I was prepared for it and adjusted the controls to counter turning into a spin. There was a tense moment as debris flew past me, and I admit I closed my eyes and prayed, hoping my suit wouldn't be punctured. The alarms in my suit didn't go off, but there was a moment of panic when Major Plural didn't respond to Sakamoto's calls. It was such a relief when I finally heard her voice again. Kelsey hadn't responded, but that's another story I'll get to in a bit.

I had to move fast as the spherical tech robots were already responding and trying to seal the blown-out doorways. I managed to push my way through and landed hard on the deck as I entered the artificial gravity environment. As I managed to get up to my feet, I noticed that, unlike the Chesty, the Jangle Berry was bright and well-lit.

"Okay, Marines." Sakamoto radioed in. "Once more, by the numbers, confirm you are on board." We all responded once more, except for Kelsey.

Suddenly there was a blast of sirens. Sakamoto came back online again. "That signals that the exits are sealed again. Head toward the bridge, but stay alert, and, for God's sake, don't accidentally shoot each other."

Even in the simulators back in training, I pulled out my snap pistol and tensed myself, ready for anything as I passed through the second door of the airlock.

I suddenly spun to my left, looking down the corridors as I heard a French voice. However, I relaxed as I saw it was a repair drone heading toward me.

It wasn't a combat model, and would happily ignore me if I didn't engage with it. However, it hung in the air, sensors looking at me for a long moment. With my gun squarely pointed at it, I waited to see what it would do, but after some babbling in French, it moved on to the door. Or rather what was left of it.

The gleaming corridor was empty as I made my way down it, heading toward what should be the bridge. I passed several bodies that were lying around in a decompressed mess. I would've felt guilty about how we killed them, if it wasn't for the bodies of fine Americans who lay on board the Lewis Puller. As I moved further down the corridor, I started to pass what looked like a laboratory with large windows looking out onto the corridor. The door was sealed air-tight shut, and I was startled to see two terrified men in white coats looking through the window, almost mindless with panic, as they came to terms with what had happened. Seeing me, they came up to the window and started to bang, clearly thinking I might be there to help them. They blathered away in French, which, obviously, I couldn't understand a word of. I stood staring at them through my helmet visor as I wondered what to do. They were enemy combatants, whatever their position was. They were a risk to our mission. I didn't know what was in that laboratory or what communications they had, but they had seen me and knew my location, and as far as I knew, they could call for some assistance to take me out.

I walked over to the door and started to press the controls as wide-eyed terror appeared on their faces, and they banged harder and screamed at me. However, the door was locked by some code and would not open for me. The men inside, realizing this, started to relax, but I simply raised my snap gun and fired a single round into the window. It was a rookie mistake. As the air rushed out of the shattering glass, it threw me back against the wall, and I slid down to the ground as my suit alarms began to go off.

"Multiple suit punctures. Recommend emergency procedures," my suit's environmental system said, stating the obvious. I pulled a can of spray sealant from my hip as I watched the air level go down in my suit's heads-up display. I pulled small pieces of glass out from various places and sprayed the holes with the swiftly hardening substance. The air depletion began to slow. It didn't stop entirely, but it was sufficient enough to get me through the rest of the mission without running out of air. I breathed a sigh of relief, and as I climbed back onto my feet, I didn't look back into that laboratory. I knew the men were dead. With no more thoughts on the matter, I ventured onward.

Over our comms, Jenna Plural and Sakamoto began discussing an issue about getting the bridge doors open without causing damage. But something else had distracted me. I came across one of the other airlocks we'd blown open and saw that Kelsey was trapped in a tangle of wires.

When she saw me, she looked relieved and spoke rapidly at me, but I couldn't hear her. She tried to point to the side of her head to indicate her communicator was out. She eagerly waited for me to get her out of the mess that she'd gotten herself into but grew concerned as I just stood there looking at her. I'm sure that I couldn't hide the contempt on my face. She had betrayed her country twice now with her cowardice, and I believed she would do so again if I allowed it. I'm sure you'll agree that I was duty-bound to ensure she didn't further endanger the rest of us with that yellow streak that ran down her back. The fact that I enjoy it is neither here, nor there. I don't falter when it comes to my responsibilities.

I stepped around behind her, and as I did, I noticed her smile again, believing that I was about to release her from her entrapment. I reached for the tube to her air supply and began to unscrew it. I then realized how silly that was, as I realized it would be problematic if she were found with her air tube simply detached. I laughed at my own stupidity, and wrapping the tube around my wrist, I yanked it hard. Kelsey started thrashing about, trying to turn around to see what I was doing. I pulled it again, getting a little frustrated now. I had much better things to be doing than this. Kelsey was just a passing irritation. In the end, I grabbed it with two hands, and lifting my foot onto her backside, I yanked it at an angle, so that even if I couldn't break the tube thread, I would at least rip the suit itself. For the life of me, I can't remember whether it was the tube or the suit, but it didn't tear completely off, just sufficiently enough to let the air out like an old bald tire.

I stepped in front of her again and watched as she silently screamed hysterically at me. Most unbecoming of a United States Marine. Even in death, she was unable to maintain her composure. I couldn't help feeling ashamed for her. The fact I couldn't hear anything was kind of disappointing. Then I turned and walked away.

As I joined Major Plural and the others on the bridge, Sakamoto desperately tried to call Kelsey. I said nothing, of course, and positioned myself near the door as Sakamoto headed out to find her. When she did, it was instantly assumed to be an accident, so all was well. The necessity of hiding what I did was not out of a sense that I was doing anything wrong. I was, however, bending the rules a little bit, but I was only doing something those snowflakes would cry about, and discretion saved a lot of paperwork. I'm absolutely sure Jenna Plural would have approved if I'd told her.

Eventually, Major Plural called over to The Puller for Grant to come and take control of the ship. After another search to ensure we were in the clear, Hardy and I returned to the Lewis Puller. My services were no longer needed, and I went to the quarters I had shared with Kelsey. I carefully packed up Kelsey's stuff and wrote a little note to her parents saying how sorry I was for their loss. After all, it wasn't their fault that their daughter was a cowardly piece of filth. Or maybe it was. Who knows, but I gave them the benefit of the doubt. I popped it into her kit bag so it would be found when her gear was sent back home.

I wasn't surprised when I later learned of the demise of the treacherous captain. Major Plural had shot him. It only enhanced my growing respect for Jenna Plural. He was blatantly a traitor, and no one can possibly deny that.

She had certainly proved herself to me that day. There was no doubt in my mind that I would die for her.

CHAPTER SEVEN

STEPHANIE MORRIS

We spent quite a bit of time working on repairs. I say working on repairs, but it was more fetching and carrying for the technicians than me doing repairs themselves. I started to feel part of the team.

Being hasty, we didn't touch the more cosmetic issues such as internal damage, and there were several holes in my quarter's walls looking out into the corridor. I was able to cover them with a picture of my brother and one of a KK Ripper, my absolute favorite firearm. Alas, I could still hear the comings and goings of people outside my quarters.

Major Plural now planned to continue our original mission to take out the central communications base on Phobos. Helen Tracker successfully patched the M.E.T., and crewmen were downloaded, but all were destined for the Phobos mission. This meant once they departed for Phobos, I would be all alone except for the Navy personnel.

It was quite disappointing that I wouldn't be a part of the assault on Phobos. I was aware that I was never part of that plan anyway, having only joined the ship as a routine personnel rotation. I wasn't a member of Jenna Plural's elite squad, and my role was little more than ship defenses and backup. But I honestly felt I could do more good down on that moon infested by the Peons.

The Jangle Berry was now a spoil of war and had been renamed the U.S.S. Lady Liberty and it was to be used to sneak into the Martian defense systems, still broadcasting as a French vessel. Stephanie Morris, the ship's first officer who had, only days before, outranked Jenna, was now subject to her orders. She was to command the Puller while Jenna took the Jangle Berry on the Phobos assault.

During this time, I was concerned I would be ordered back into the M.E.T. and I kept as low a profile as my duties permitted, usually eating meals when no-one else was around. On this particular day, I walked in on Morris seated in the mess.

"My apologies, M...M...Ma'am," I said quickly, and I made to step out.

"No, no, come in, Marine," she said, beckoning me in. I didn't want to. I wanted to go back to my room and wait until she left, but she was an officer, even if she had been removed from office. I stepped in and stood in the attention position. "I just made fresh coffee if you want some," she said, smiling at me and indicating the pot on the counter.

"Thank you, ma'am," I said and stepped over to the counter to pour myself a cup. Then I turned with pot in hand and asked, "Would you l...like a refresh, m...Ma'am?"

"Thank you, Private...," she said questioningly, pushing her cup toward me, indicating that she wanted to know my name.

"D...D...Dodgson, Ma'am," I replied as I refilled her cup. I returned the jug to the coffee maker and stood there holding my own, unsure of what to do next.

She smiled at me. I noticed a glistening in her eyes as if she had been crying. "Please take a seat, Dodgson."

I still didn't want to; I still just wanted to leave. However, an officer is an officer. So I took a seat in the chair adjacent to her but remained sitting formally.

"How are your preparations for the Phobos mission going?" She asked.

"I understand they're g...g...going well," I replied. "However, I won't be p...p...part of that mission, unfortunately," I explained.

"Oh, why not?"

"It was n...never intended that I be d...downloaded, Ma'am. I only joined the ship after Lieutenant P...P...Plural had put her t...team together."

I felt uneasy telling her about that as I thought her immediate response would be that I should instantly be uploaded again.

"You sound disappointed about that?"

"I'm a M...M...Marine, ma'am." I sighed. "It's what I t...t...trained for. It's who I am."

"Well, technically, the war is over now," she replied, trying to sound casual, but failed dismally. "We should be going home."

I wasn't sure how to respond to this as I didn't know the intent behind the statement. Yeah, she was technically right, but was she just making a statement, or was she expressing opposition to Major Plural? In the end, all I said was, "Yes, m...Ma'am."

There was an uneasy pause that made me uncomfortable. "Where are you from, Dodgson?" She eventually asked.

"Arizona, Ma'am. A t...town called Sedona."

Morris smiled. "A beautiful town. I went there on vacation once while visiting the Grand Canyon."

"Yes, ma'am, its main industry is t...tourism," I said formally, unsure of where she was going.

"Do you miss it?"

"Ma'am, I only just joined the s...ship immediately before this mission. I...I haven't been gone long enough to m...m...miss it yet," I replied.

She pondered my words, and I tried to make out the meaning of her expression as she studied me and thought about what I had just said. "So you haven't worked with Jenna Plural prior to us leaving Earth on this occasion?" She asked eventually.

"No, ma'am."

"What do you think of our current situation?"

"Well, to be honest, it s...sucks, Ma'am." I suddenly found myself venting my frustrations from the past week. A surprising quirk of my speech condition was how I lost my stammer when extremely pissed off. "I don't know how she thinks she has a right to make this decision. It affects all of us, and there's been no consideration as to how we feel about it. She's going to lead us all to our deaths." I suddenly noticed how Morris was staring at me, and I realized that I may have gone too far in my contempt for the President. But what the hell? I had voted for her on her 'never surrender' policy, and she had screwed me and every other American right up the ass. I calmed myself and looked away. "I'm sorry, Ma'am, that was m...most ina...pr...propriate of me."

To my surprise, she reached out and placed her hand inappropriately upon mine.

"It's okay, Dodgson," she said reassuringly. "You're not alone in how you feel." She then appeared to change the subject. "I'll be assuming command of the Lewis Puller during the Phobos mission. Once Lieutenant Plural's team has transferred to the European ship, I want you to come and see me on the bridge."

"Yes, M...ma'am," I said, curious about what she wanted with me. With that, she took her leave, not having even touched the coffee I had poured for her.

"I'll see you then." She said quite warmly as she got up.

As she reached the door, I found myself saying, "Ma'am, it's M...M...Major Plural now."

"What?" She looked confused for a moment.

"It's Major P...P...Plural now, not Lieutenant."

She hesitated once more, before smiling and saying, "Yes, Dodgson, of course, it is."

And with that, she left. I thought nothing more of it and finished my coffee before making myself a sandwich and returning to my room.

******

A couple of days later, Major Plural had her Phobos team transferred to The Lady Liberty. I felt another pang of disappointment as I watched them cross over to the ship and the airlock sealed behind them.

I wanted to watch them depart, but the only window was on the bridge, and I wasn't quite ready to meet with Lieutenant Morris again. I returned to my quarters, took a shower, and donned a fresh uniform before heading to see her.

There was a new pilot at the helm. Or rather, I should say an old pilot at the helm, although he wasn't old. I just mean that he was the pilot prior to Stacey Grant joining the ship. I personally thought it was a disgrace that a foreigner should be allowed the privileged position of a United States Officer and command Americans. I was sure Batty was surely the better pilot than some uncultured Australian that served in a second-rate air force.

Neville Batty was a lively little guy with a cheerful disposition. Instead of returning my salute as I entered the bridge, he remained in his seat and just gave me a little wave like he was passing me in a car on a sunny afternoon in Central Park. Yes, I know you don't drive around Central Park. I just wanted to give it a more colorful metaphor.

Morris was seated in the captain's chair and smiled at me as I entered. "Ah yes, Dobson, isn't it?"

"Dodgson, Ma'am," I said, hiding my irritation.

"Oh yes, Dodgson, sorry." She sounded genuinely apologetic.

"Not a problem, Ma'am. Everybody does it," I stated professionally.

"That doesn't make it right, Dodgson."

I smiled. Maybe she wasn't that bad after all. She turned her attention back to Batty. "How long is it been since the Lady Liberty departed?"

"About thirty minutes, ma'am."

Stephanie smiled and carefully stepped out of her seat. "You have the bridge, Lieutenant Batty."

"Aye, Ma'am."

"With me, Dodgson." And I followed her out on her heels.

I had no idea where she was taking me and was surprised when we ended up in the M.E.T. room. For a moment, I thought she was going to upload me, but as we stepped inside, I saw there was a young tech who wasn't Helen Tracker. She had left on the Phobos mission with Major Plural.

"Private Dodgson, this is Assistant Technician Sinclair." Morris introduced. "Is everything ready, Miss Sinclair?" She asked her.

"Yes, ma'am, I've isolated his matrix," she smiled sweetly.

"Very good, bring him down." As Morris said this, I instinctively closed my eyes to avoid the flash of light. A tall, handsome young man stood before me when I opened them. I turned away quickly to face the wall, completely forgetting that you come out of the M.E.T. buck naked. I listened to his conversation with Morris as she handed him his uniform and he started to dress.

"What is going on, Stephanie?" He said, sounding confused.

"I have a lot to tell you, Frankie," Morris said.

It turned out that Frank Mitchell was a security officer in the Navy. He had worked alongside Stephanie Morris for several years and had just transferred to the Lewis Puller. Stephanie related the events of the ship's boarding and the United States' surrender.

Naturally, he was in a state of shock. He didn't know how to respond to that, and she gave him a moment to adjust as I finally turned round to see the fully dressed, able seaman. I noticed how relaxed Sinclair was as Morris spoke, and I realized that she already knew what was going on. I was completely shocked by what Morris said next.

"Jenna Plural has gone insane. She murdered the captain and has assumed control." Morris stated. I admit I was taken aback by this statement, but held back my fervent desire to protest.

Mitchell was startled by this news, but I noticed again how Sinclair took that news in her stride. She was clearly in cahoots with whatever Morris was now up to. "Jenna has left the ship with her cronies. Unless we want to end up dead along with her, we have no alternative but to take action."

Mitchell looked at me, then questioningly at Morris. The fact that he didn't look at Sinclair with the same unspoken question clearly meant he already knew where her loyalties lay.

"This is Dodgson," Morris said. "She's new and a loyal United States Marine Corps member and shares our concerns about Plural." I had no clue what could have given her that idea, but now was not the time to say anything.

"I've brought her in as my personal guard, as I don't know how the crew will respond."

Mitchell smiled at me and extended a hand. I maintained my composure, as I was still trying to figure out this turn of events in my head. I smiled as warmly as possible and took his hand.

"Hi there, Dobson. I'm Chief Petty Officer Frank Mitchell. I'm the ship's head of security, and I look forward to working with you." He was so charming and kind, but then, the Devil is the great deceiver, isn't he?

"Likewise, chief," I said with my sweetest smile.

He turned to Morris.

"Are there any of her people still remaining? That Gen-Mod has an almost fanatical loyalty among her minions," he said contemptuously.

"Well, there is Rock Harlow, the chief engineer. However, he's quite elderly now. I doubt he put up much of a fight. I don't know why Jenna got him posted to this ship. He should have retired years ago."

"Yeah, the most you'll get from Harlow is a few grunts of disapproval at the worst," Sinclair chuckled.

"Neville Batty is quite a wild card," Morris continued. "He's worked with Jenna for the last four years, but Stacey Grant replaced him as chief pilot at her instruction, so who knows? He does seem enamored by her."

"It's more like Neville is thinking with his dick," Sinclair grinned. "He has the hots for anyone with a slim waistline, and there's no denying Jenna Plural is probably the sexiest thing he's ever seen."

Sinclair was cute with a pale, daintily youthful face and was short and petite, and I have to admit that I was very attracted to her.

"Well, it's not like we can magic up another pilot," Mitchell sighed. "We'll just have to make sure we keep an eye on him."

Morris smiled, and she stepped up close to him, and I thought for a moment she was going to kiss him. However, he glanced over at me, and then so did she. Somewhat embarrassed, she stepped back. I did my best to act as if I hadn't noticed anything, and Morris smiled appreciatively at me for it.

I didn't know what I'd walked into at this point, but I really didn't like it. Not only did it appear that Stephanie Morris was about to betray Major Plural, but she was also fraternizing with an enlisted man who was supposed to be her security officer!

"There *is* some bad news," Sinclair said. "Tracker has the computer systems encoded with an algorithm that is way beyond my ability to even understand, let alone override. I did ponder talking to her about the situation, because I believe it may have been possible to persuade her to throw in with us. I know she has issues with Jenna's ethics. However, Plural kept us so busy that I didn't get a chance to be alone with her."

Morris sighed.

"Well, it's academic now, as Tracker is on Phobos and will remain there until the Peons pick her up." I couldn't help but audibly react to this. Morris turned toward me. "Yes, I know it absolutely sucks, but I have a duty to those

I can actually help. Plural will lead those people to their deaths, and it's my duty to ensure that I can save as many as possible from her insanity."

It was far too dangerous at this point for me to disagree. I decided to see how this would play out and simply replied, "I understand, M...ma'am. It's just that I like Helen T...Tracker." Fuck, I didn't even really know Helen Tracker at this point in time.

They seemed to accept what I'd said as Mitchell grinned at me.

"It's impossible not to like Helen Tracker. She is such a sweetheart. However, the commander here is right. It's not like we can take on Jenna Plural's Marines even if we wanted to. For all her failings, her reputation as one of the greatest tacticians in history is not without merit."

"Okay, let's do this!" Morris steeled herself. "You and Dodgson go to the armory. Make sure you at least have sidearms at all times. Sinclair and I will head up to the bridge and meet you there."

The four of us headed out and went in separate directions. I followed behind Mitchell as we made our way to the armory. I considered taking him out then and there. Step up behind him, throw an arm around his neck, a quick twist, and drop him. Adios motherfucker. But what then? Go up to the bridge with a snap pistol blazing away? If Batty sided with Morris, I was up shit creek without a paddle. I couldn't fly the damn ship.

No, this was a game of patience, and I needed to see where this was going. Mitchell cheerfully chatted with me and asked me questions about my background, and once more, I had to explain my speech impediment, which I politely answered in my usual sweet and friendly manner.

Being chief of security, he had the access codes to the armory. Now, this was Nirvana to me. To be surrounded by all these tools of annihilation, I just wanted to hug each and every rifle, explosive, and blade. Alas, Mitchell removed two snap pistols from a rack and handed one to me with a spare clip.

"These are only for last resort, Dobson," he said very carefully. "The whole objective here is to save lives, not take them."

"Yes, ch...Chief," I said, and to be quite honest, he was absolutely right. The sanctity of the patriotic American lives was absolute – of course, there were exceptions – and Morris and her foul, treasonous ilk were in the latter category.

Together, we headed back up to the bridge.

CHAPTER EIGHT

WORKING FOR THE ENEMY

Morris was back in the command seat, and Sinclair stood at her side as we re-entered the cockpit. "The Lady Liberty has advised us that they have successfully disabled the Phobos minefield," Sinclair told us.

"Excellent," Mitchell said as he slipped into the co-pilot chair next to Batty. "Hey Neville, how are you doing, buddy?"

"Hey Mitch," Batty gave him a beaming smile. "Good to see you, bud. It's been a while."

Mitchell laughed. "Hey, it's only been a day for me. I'm starting to think I'll spend the rest of my life in an M.E.T.."

Batty chuckled. "Yeah, I know what you mean. Ever since Stacey took my place as the senior pilot, I've felt like a spare part in storage."

"We should put in for a transfer to a bigger ship when everything is over, so we don't spend so much time not existing." Mitchell laughed and then turned to Morris and asked, "Any chance of any coffee, Ma'am?"

Morris smiled at him, a little too warmly for my liking, and then looked up at me and said, "Would you be a dear?"

Be a dear? Did she really just call me that? However, I nodded, returned her smile, and said, "Yes, Ma'am."

I headed back down to the mess, where I made a pot of coffee and pondered if there was anything I could put in it to take them out. I didn't know how deep this ran, and I couldn't risk harming Batty, the only pilot aboard. So, disappointed, I returned to the bridge with a tray of mugs and a pot of regular coffee, and poured it out for everyone in turn, handing it out like a steward.

Morris dismissed Sinclair and me, asking us to report back in a couple of hours. As we both left, I walked alongside Sinclair and couldn't help but notice in my peripheral vision that she kept stealing glances at me. Eventually, I asked, "Is something on your mind, Sinclair?"

"Sorry," she said sheepishly. "I was just thinking...you know..." Her voice trailed off, and she looked uncomfortable.

I didn't know. I stopped walking and turned to face her. "Say what you w...w...want to."

"Please call me Paris."

I frowned, "W...why? "

She looked surprised by my question, and then laughed a rather delightful little laugh. "Because that's my name. Paris Sinclair."

"Oh, I see. I'm sorry." Then I added, "That's rather an unfortunate n....n...name, given our circumstances, don't you think?"

She laughed. "You're not the first person to comment on that."

Why any American would ever call their daughter Paris or any other French name was beyond my comprehension. Could it be this was why she was so easily led astray?

"Look," she said, steeling herself. "You know...um, you're kind of cute. I was wondering... uh, after all this is over, maybe we could have a drink together or something?"

My reaction to this was confused. I was aware that I was attracted to women as much as I was to men, but being raised in a strictly devout family had made me feel tremendously guilty about it. But, standing in front of me, looking so nervous and sweet at the same time, I felt the desire to pull her to me and give her a great big hug. I had to remind myself that she'd made herself an enemy of Jenna Plural, who was now America's last great hope. Duty before desire. Semper Fi.

What I said was, "I appreciate the compliment, P...P...Paris, and I'd be happy to have a drink with you as f...f...friends. But anything more isn't really my inclination."

She looked disappointed, but she smiled.

"That is possibly the sweetest rejection I've ever had." She laughed. She had such an adorable smile, and I was saddened that I would eventually have to rip it off her face.

I placed a reassuring hand on her shoulder and replied. "Don't worry. I took it as a c...compliment." I then went to my cabin, telling her I would see her later.

I spent the next couple of days trying to come up with some sort of plan. I couldn't call Major Plural, and I couldn't take over the ship without a visit to an Air Force flight school. When it became time for me to return to the bridge, I still had nothing.

Sinclair was already there, and there was heightened tension emanating from both Morris and Mitchell. As I stepped in, Morris advised me, "Plural has landed. They are engaging the enemy, and the Liberty is on course for a mission to get a new air supply."

"So what are w...w...we doing?" I asked. My hand casually slipped down to my holster and over the grip of my snap pistol, getting ready to draw it, should I need to.

"Let's let Stacey get further away before we do anything," said Mitchell, and Batty looked up confused, but when no-one said anything to him, he kind of shrugged and looked back at his console.

We stood there in silence for what felt like forever, but it was probably only an hour. Mitchell turned to Morris, and she nodded to him. He got out of his chair and casually stood behind Batty, and I watched him slip his hand down to his snap gun. I moved to the doorway so no-one could see me unless they turned around, and I gripped my snap gun, too, ready to pull it out should he do anything to harm Batty.

"Fire up the engines, Mr. Batty, and bring us about," Morris ordered, and he automatically complied. It was not a pilot's place to question the commanding officer, but what she said next made him turn around. "Plot a course for Earth and set us to maximum speed."

He spun around in his seat. "Are you sure, ma'am?" He asked with wide, confused eyes.

"You heard the captain, Mr. Batty. Please don't question her authority," said Mitchell, but he relaxed as Batty frowned, then shrugged and turned to plot the course.

"Course set in. E.T.A. seven weeks and four days," Batty reported uneasily.

"Thank you, Mr. Batty," Morris said cheerfully.

And there it was. There was no doubting it now. Stephanie Morris had just abandoned Major Plural and her Marines on Phobos and was about to turn us over to the enemy forces. My mind raced on what to do. I didn't even know who among the crew I could trust anymore.

"Mr. Mitchell, would you please give Mr. Batty that frequency we discussed so he can call her up," Morris ordered.

Mitchell slipped a piece of paper out of his pocket and slid it across the console to Batty. He looked at it, then looked up at Mitchell, then at Morris, and then patched the call to the frequency provided.

"Taggart here." Came the voice of an unfamiliar woman over the radio.

"Corporal Taggart, it is good to hear your voice again," Morris said cheerfully.

"Likewise, Lieutenant. I was starting to worry I wouldn't hear from you. How is everything going over there?"

"We've taken the Lewis Puller," Morris said with pride. "Now it's up to you to take The Liberty. Did you manage to recruit any of your colleagues into our mission?"

"No, ma'am. I'm on my own, but I've incapacitated the two Marines with me. That leaves Grant, her tech, and Pentauk."

"I would rather there was no bloodshed, but if you have no choice, you'll have to take out Stacey Grant and the others. Are you willing to do that?"

There was a barely audible laugh as Taggart replied, "Willing to take out Stacey Grant? Hell, I'd actually enjoy it."

"Only if absolutely necessary, Corporal Taggart," Morris instructed. "You want to place her under arrest if at all possible. Do we understand each other?"

"Yes, of course," Taggart said with frustration. "I'll call you again once I have control."

I'm not exactly the biggest fan of that slut Stacey Grant, but at least at this point, I knew she was as loyal as any foreigner could be. There was no way I wanted her to be killed. Well, at least not back then. That would obviously change, but she was on my side right now, and I possibly needed her. Desperate times and all that. However, I was in an impossible situation. Even if I took out Morris, Mitchell, and Sinclair right now, that wouldn't stop this Taggart.

"Okay, what the fuck is going on?" Batty made to jump out of his seat, but Mitchell pushed him back down again from the shoulder.

"Trust me, Mr. Batty, I am trying to save all our lives," replied Morris.

"Killing one of my best friends doesn't sound like trying to save lives!" Batty protested. I assume he referred to Grant, but I couldn't imagine her having friends. At least not American ones.

"That will be the decision of Stacey herself. No harm will come to her if she stands down and recognizes my command," Morris replied. "But I must consider the greater good of the many lives I could save."

"And Mr. Batty," said Mitchell. "I don't want to hurt you, but you've already laid in the course for the Earth, and who's going to control the ship won't become a problem for seven weeks. We can do without you, but we'd rather not."

"This is fucking bullshit," he muttered, turning back to the controls with resignation. He almost immediately looked back up at Morris. "We have a call coming in from the Liberty."

"Put it on speaker," Morris ordered.

That crudely accented voice that would eventually grate on my nerves came over the tannoy system. "This is Stacey Grant of the U.S.S. Lady Liberty, to the U.S.S. Lewis Puller. Do you read me?"

Mitchell looked back at Morris, concern on his face. She sighed dejectedly and shook her head slowly before responding. "This is Morris. Go ahead, Miss Grant."

"I don't know what you're playing at, mate, but your little coup here has just failed." There was a sigh from the jezebel before she continued. "I want you to listen very carefully." Morris did not respond, so Grant repeated. "Are you listening?"

"Yes!"

There was a long pause, and then suddenly, the sound of a snap gun going off, followed by a dull thud before the Australian's voice came back, filled with frustration. "Do you know what that was, Stephanie? That was the former Corporal Taggart dying. I didn't want to do that, but I don't have the resources here to take prisoners."

I could't help but smile, but I hid it quickly before anyone noticed. Batty was less discreet. "You go, Stacey," he muttered with a grin.

"Listen to me, Stacey," Morris said steadily and firmly, but I could see her shaking slightly. "You have to know that Jenna Plural is power crazy. She's out of her freaking mind! Do you really think she and a handful of United States Marines could take on the whole solar system? Do you think you're going to fly the Lewis Puller into Canberra and liberate Australia? Listen to how stupid that is."

"You're probably entirely correct," Stacey replied. "However, I'd rather go out taking as many of those fuckers with me, than stick my head between my knees and kiss my arse and the arse of the nearest Peon." There was a pause. "We'll be coming for you. That's something I'm sure'll be Jenna's first order upon her return."

And with that, the line went dead.

I looked at Morris, who had her elbow resting on the arm of the chair and was biting her thumbnail, thinking out what to do next.

"If she finds a way to get Plural off that moon, they'll be coming after us," Mitchell said urgently. "We can't outrun the Liberty, *and* she'll have an almost complete squad of United States Marines with her."

"All we can do is hope Grant isn't successful with her mission to the Peon space station," Morris muttered.

"That's leaving a lot to chance, Stephanie. We have to find a way to ensure that they don't come after us." Mitchell insisted.

Morris sighed, looked up at the ceiling, then dejectedly, she looked to Batty. "Call up the Peon space station she's heading for."

Batty turned in his seat and raised his eyebrows. "Excuse me?"

"You heard me, Mr. Batty. Please, let's not make this worse than it already is."

Batty turned back, tapped in the frequencies, and violently hit the control. "You have an open line, Captain," he said to the captain with deliberate contempt.

"This is the U.S.S. Lewis Puller to European base blah blah." Obviously, she didn't say 'blah blah,' but I can't remember whatever silly name they had for it. Someone responded in French, but moments later, someone speaking pretty reasonable English for a Peon came online.

"How can we help you, mademoiselle?" Although the words were polite, there was clear suspicion in his voice. There may have been a peace called, but that didn't end twenty years of suspicion.

"This is Captain Stephanie Morris of the U.S.S. Lewis Puller. There is a ship headed toward you with the transponder codes for a ship in your fleet called the Jangle Berry." She said the proper French name for the ship, of course. "It's under the control of an Australian renegade. She intends to take your base by force in order to obtain your supplies."

There was a pause before he replied. "If this is so, then why would you tell me? You are American."

"This is a rogue element. This is not an officially sanctioned United States action."

Again, there was another pause before he reluctantly said, "Very well, we will take it under advisement."

Morris was about to say something else, but Batty advised her they had cut the line.

"I felt dirty doing that, but it was for the best," she muttered. Standing behind her, I struggled not to show the bare, unadulterated anger seething through my body.

As time passed after communicating with Stacey, I almost fell into despair.

I slept late the next day. Any former military protocol had gone out the window, and no-one assigned me any duties. I woke with a start when Sinclair came banging on my door.

"Somehow, Plural has escaped Phobos with the help of Stacey Grant. The Liberty is coming after us."

My heart skipped an excited beat, but I hid my joy well. "Will they catch up before we get to Earth?"

"According to Batty, they'll overtake us in just a few more days. Apparently, they've been following for quite a while, but he managed to hide their signature from us, the little shithead."

Good old Neville Batty. American heroes come in all shapes and sizes, and from all walks of life. You don't have to be a frontline combat veteran to be a hero.

But it certainly helps.

Chapter Nine

Justice is Served

An opportunity to take out Morris still didn't arise, and I became increasingly frustrated as the next few days passed. There were many meetings held that I attended. Sinclair reported she had managed a workaround on the M.E.T., and it was finally decided that they would start downloading the remaining Marines to repel any attempt to board from The Lady Liberty.

Something I could not let happen. So, one evening, I stopped off at the M.E.T. room, opened up the control panel, and pulled out a couple of wires, hoping that I wasn't going to cause harm to those inside. However, desperate times call for desperate measures, as I've said before. Hopefully, the traitors would think it was related to the previous damage caused during Lieutenant Plural's takeover of the Chesty. Job done.

As The Liberty started to pull in for the attack, Sinclair went to begin the downloads. She quickly reported the fault to the captain, so I kindly offered to go down and help her. She was flustered as she tried to work out what was wrong. When she opened up the casing, she frowned.

"Fucking hell!" She cursed. "This isn't accidental! Someone's sabotaged this."

"Can you f...fix it?" I asked, hoping for a negative answer.

"Oh sure! It'll only take two minutes," she said brightly.

Damn it! I really liked Paris Sinclair, and it was such a shame.

"I was h...hoping you weren't going to say th...that," I said softly.

She turned to face me with a confused expression. "Huh?"

I slammed the palm of my hand against her face and smashed her head back against the wall with considerable force. Unfortunately, I couldn't shoot or stab her because that would leave a nasty mess they could find.

She screamed in pain and fear, and I placed my hand over her mouth and slammed her head several more times before realizing that, if I split her skull open, that would make a mess too. She looked up at me in a dazed shock and tried to say something that sounded like, 'Why?' but I couldn't honestly be sure. I placed my other hand around her neck and dragged her down onto the ground as she thrashed about, trying to kick and scratch at me, but I managed to force her head down and knelt a knee upon her back. I pondered various ways that I could draw this experience out. However, nothing occurred to me that wouldn't involve opening up a vein or an artery, and the practicality of time left me quite disappointed. Her soft moans and sobs were quite arousing. There really wasn't time for any fun.

So, with much regret, I placed my fingers around her forehead and yanked her head back forcefully until I heard the sound of bone and cartilage cracking in her neck, and she fell silent.

One down, two to go.

I dragged her body out of the room, and half lifting and half carrying, I took her to a seldom-used storage closet .*** It wouldn't be used, at least, until this situation was resolved. Ironically, it turned out no one ever found her, and I would later put her body into the garbage regularly ejected into space. With justice served on Paris Sinclair and no backup arriving from the M.E.T., I headed back up to the bridge.

Morris looked nervous, clammy, and pale, which both delighted and disgusted me. "How is Sinclair doing?" She asked me.

"She seems to be doing okay," I replied. "However, she said she couldn't concentrate with me there and asked for everyone to leave her alone."

"Get back down there and tell her I want a solid timeline on when we'll be able to download our troops."

I nodded and went to sit in the mess room for ten minutes, drinking a cup of coffee before returning to report my findings. I walked in just as she was finishing a conversation with Major Plural on the radio.

"You've had your chance to surrender, Morris," Major Plural said. "Your time is up. When we next meet each other, my face will be the last one you see. Liberty out."

The eyes of myself, Batty, and Mitchell were all on Stephanie Morris. She was visibly shaking now, but no commands came from her.

"What are your orders, Captain?" Mitchell asked.

A deathly silence hung aboard the ship until a clang rang through the ship, and those of us standing almost lost our balance.

"Wow, Stacey is just going to do a bounce grapple on us. Color me impressed," laughed Batty, but neither Stephanie, nor Mitchell were amused.

"We have to get out of here, Mitchell!" Morris jumped up from her seat. "Take our chances in a life pod. Jenna is not going to let this go. We're both dead if she gets back aboard this ship." She looked at me. "You should come too. I don't think 'I was only obeying orders' will cut any ice with that psychopath."

I nodded and followed both Mitchell and Morris out of the bridge.

If I was going to do something, I was severely running out of time. I did wonder if I should just wait for Major Plural to board, but if Morris got into an escape capsule, there was no way the two ships could disentangle in time to pursue her, and there was no way I was going to let her walk away from this. Such a thing would be un-American. I only had as long as it took to walk from the front of the ship to the back to do something.

Major Plural's voice came on the ship-wide intercom.

"This is Major Jenna Plural of the Lady Liberty. We already have control of the Chesty, and I am ordering you all to stand down. This is your chance to be patriots, ladies and gentlemen. Stand down and place Stephanie Morris under arrest!"

She clearly had no clue I had prevented the download of troops who could possibly be loyal to Morris – unbelievable as that may be.

This was it. I had to do something now. I removed my snap pistol from my holster as we turned a corner. I started to raise it toward the back of Morris' head, but as bad luck would have it, Mitchell turned around to say something to me just at that moment. His eyes widened, but at the same time, he swiped my arm, and the snap gun fired off into the wall. Morris barely glanced back and ran around the corner. Mitchell grabbed my arm and banged it against the wall until I dropped the weapon. I tried to bring my knee up into his groin, but he managed to step back without letting go of me. He then twisted my arm, causing me to turn around, and had every intention of breaking it. I managed to bring the heel of my boot back against his shin. Hardly enough to do anything, other than give him a nasty bruise, but sufficient to distract him momentarily. I broke free, spun around, and punched him squarely in the mouth. I don't know whom it hurt more, him or me, but the fight was on.

I followed up with a head butt busting the bridge of his nose, but in an unexpected move, his hands went for my neck and latched on. Try as I might to avoid it, it's the automatic instinct of a human to go for the hands that are choking it. And I did just that. A fruitless and pointless move as I began to soundlessly gag under the pressure of his thumbs as they were squeezing the life out of me. Fortunately, my training came to me as he forced me to the ground and landed on top of me. With all the strength I could muster, I rammed my forefinger into his eye and kept it going up to the knuckle. The weird sucking sound as I pulled my finger out was barely audible above his screams. He clutched at his face, and I tried to heave him off of me as blood and slime poured from his eye socket down onto my face.

It took a while to get him off me, and I scrambled up to my feet as he flailed out at me. I brought my boot down onto the side of his head, stamping down several times harder and harder until he fell silent and stopped moving. He was dead, but I didn't know it, for I had no time to check.

I pulled his security cuffs from his belt, snatched up my gun, and ran faster than ever. My old drill Sergeant would have had nothing to complain about this time.

Morris was climbing into one of the escape pods as I entered the bay. I stepped up to her and angrily raised my snap pistol to her head.

"Please stop what you're doing, Ma'am. Major wants you alive, but I *will* shoot you if I have to."

She turned around and raised her hands. "What made you change sides?"

"I never switched sides. There's always only been one side, Ma'am."

"But back in the mess that day, you said Jenna had no right and was leading us to our deaths!"

I stared back at her with wide-eyed disbelief. "I was talking about the goddamn president. Not Jenna Plural. For fuck's sake, Ma'am!" I was screaming now. "Jenna Plural is our only hope! And I for one, am not going to roll over and play dead like you! I'm not giving up on America and the American dream."

"Oh my God, you're as insane as she is..." Morris muttered.

"Insanity is th...thinking you could g...g...get away with this. Victory is, and always will be, the d...destiny of the American people. Now g...get out of there." She followed the direction of where I pointed the gun. "T...turn around and hands against the wall. Move so much as an inch, and I w...will shoot you."

"That would probably be better than whatever Jenna Plural has planned for me," She responded curtly.

I shrugged, allowing myself to calm down. "Shooting you in the n...n...kneecap is not going to k...kill you," I said coldly, and she quickly complied.

I remembered the cuffs I took from Mitchell and cuffed her to a pipe. I then went to wash my face and hands before I walked over to the intercom. I took a deep breath.

"Batty, would you kindly give me a line to the Lady Liberty, please?"

"Why?" He asked suspiciously.

"I have i...information that Major Plural will want to know." He still didn't trust me, but he complied.

I heard the beep to say the line was open, and very nervously, I said, "This is P...private Emma Dodgson. I have Commander Morris in custody, and she's really mad."

There was a pause, and I smiled as I heard cheering and clapping coming over the line, and then...*she* spoke to me.

"I think I love you, Private Dodgson," Major Plural said. I felt a warm sensation of pride at her words.

"Um, I g...guess that's appreciated, Ma'am," I said, trying to sound professional.

"Clear the portside. We're coming aboard." She instructed.

"Aye, Ma'am."

Eventually, Hardy would arrive and take charge of the prisoner. He was a lot rougher with her than I would've been, and I noticed he had a big roll of cable over his shoulder and wondered what it was for. As I trotted on behind them, I admit I found it all quite exciting.

We went into the cargo bay and were soon joined by Major Plural and Mr. Phelkar. Stephanie Morris stood in the center of the room, her hands now bound behind her back. She struggled to maintain her composure, but the terror was clear in her eyes. Major Plural walked straight up to her and slapped her hard around the face.

"You disgust me."

It was such a joy to see my leader – the future of the American people – so strong, so powerful, and so in charge. Whatever my feelings were for her before, I now realized how much I respected her, and as she slapped Morris, I couldn't help but give a little gasp of pleasure. Mr. Phelkar, always the perfect gentleman, thought the scene was bothering me and turned to me and whispered, "Do you want to wait outside?" I declined his kind offer and stood resolutely, ensuring that I made no more such outbursts.

"Look, Jenna," Morris said between anguished sobs. "You don't need to do this. Let's just talk about it. Let me out of here, and I will follow you anywhere you want. I'll accept your authority."

Major Plural folded her arms and paced up and down in front of her.

"You're a complete coward, aren't you?" She said with bile in her tone. "You think I'll just sit back and forget your actions? You tried to turn me in to the damn Peons!"

Morris began visibly shaking, and Major Plural suddenly stepped back in horror as a wet patch appeared on her crotch and spread down her thighs. She was so afraid she had peed herself. She defaced the uniform of a United States Marine. A uniform, I should say, she should never have been allowed to wear.

"String her up," the Major bluntly instructed Hardy.

Hardy nodded. He threw the cable over a beam in front of the former First Officer, and I saw it had been formed into a slipknot.

"Let's leave him to it," Mr. Phelkar said to me, but Major Plural thought he was talking to her.

She shook her head. "You can leave if you want to, but I promised Morris that I would be the last thing she sees, and unlike her, I won't be faithless."

And there was no way I would miss seeing this foul traitor dispatched. Tears streamed down Stephanie Morris's face, and I went over to help her to stand, for she buckled at the knees as Malcolm put the noose around her neck. She looked at me with eyes pleading with me to help her.

"Raise her slowly!" Major Plural commanded and moved directly in front of her, her hands behind her back and legs astride. Malcolm nodded and pulled her slowly up about half a foot from the ground. As the tips of her toes left the ground, Stephanie Morris's legs began to kick and thrash, unable to do anything with her bound hands. Her face quickly turned red as the cable bit into her throat, cutting off her air. Phelkar, a sensitive soul, turned away, but Major Plural and the rest of us watched.

We remained there in silence for several minutes as Morris continued to struggle. I was so disappointed when Major Plural sighed and pulled out her sidearm. She shot her squarely in the chest. She really did not deserve that mercy. Morris momentarily stiffened and then fell limp as the front of her shirt turned red. Major Plural remained, staring at her for a full minute. Then, turning away, she strode to the door without looking back, muttering the order, "Throw her out of an airlock."

As I watched her go, I truly realized she was our new savior.

CHAPTER TEN

THE MARK OF JENNA

I was summoned to Major Plural's office the next day. I wanted to change into a fresh uniform, but with the events of the last few days, I didn't have any. I was pretty much wearing my last decent set. As I raced up to her office, my heart was pounding. What could she possibly want? Had they found the body of Sinclair? I was yet to dispose of it at this point. I often wonder why that bothered me so much. I could certainly justify killing her. I guess it was just becoming a habit.

When I entered her office, I stood at attention until she permitted me to stand down, and she rose from behind her desk with a big smile as she moved around to stand before me.

"Lieutenant Dobson, isn't it?"

"D...Dodgson, ma'am."

"Oh, I'm sorry, Private Dodgson. I wanted to thank you for your sterling work. You truly showed your loyalty, and I have a lot of respect for that. I assume you were also responsible for Mr. Mitchell?"

"He gave me no choice, Ma'am. He tried to stop me from arresting Lieutenant Morris."

Major Plural laughed lightly and raised a reassuring hand.

"Relax, Dodgson. I'm not conducting an inquiry. I wanted to commend you. For conduct above and beyond the call of duty. And for bravery in the face of the enemy, but most of all, for making the right decision and showing me your loyalty. I shan't forget that Dodgson." She fixed those bright blue eyes on me. "You're one of my team now, and in time, I hope I'll be able to show the same loyalty to you as you've shown me." She offered me her hand to shake, and I took it. It was so soft and smooth. A chill ran down my spine, and the thought of her taking me into her arms was overwhelming.

"I...it's an honor and a p...privilege, Ma'am," I said meekly.

She smiled. "The honor and privilege are mine, Dodgson. You are hereby promoted to the rank of corporal." She returned to her desk and, sitting back, she arched her fingers and stared at me a while longer. "Mr. Phelkar requires a personal assistant, not a job I would usually give to a combat veteran, but it's not like we brought clerical staff on this trip, and new circumstances require us to adapt."

"Mr. Phelkar seems to be a very n...nice man. I will do my best t...to assist him," I replied.

She smiled again. "I am sure you will, Corporal Dodgson. If you ever need anything, my door is always open. Dismissed."

With that, I clicked my heels together and saluted. She stood up and returned the salute, and I left her office. However, as I stepped outside, two of my fellow Marines blocked my way. I looked up at them, confused. They clearly wouldn't let me pass, yet they were grinning at me. It was Neuman, the tech who also passed as an incredibly competent cook. Someone I'd seen at the arrival party in the mess was at his side, but I didn't know his name then. It was Lawson. However, what was most odd was that they were both grinning at me. I felt incredibly uncomfortable and turned back to look at Major Plural questioningly.

She was standing up, albeit still behind her desk, with her hands behind her back and a beaming smile in my direction. She feigned an innocent look at me and said in an equally fake innocent voice, "Oh did I forget to mention I'm also making you a member of Theta squad? Just because I have you doing paperwork, doesn't mean to say you can't be part of the most elite team in the solar system." The surprise on my face must have been most amusing, for she laughed as she stepped around at the table. "Like I said, Dodgson, I'm loyal to those who show their loyalty to me. I said you were now part of my team."

I can't explain the feelings that I was going through ... euphoria, exhilaration, pride. I tried to say something but found the words wouldn't come.

Jenna looked momentarily concerned and asked me, "Are you alright, Dodgson?"

"I'm...completely speechless, Ma'am."

I turned to look at the two men, still grinning like idiots and showing no signs of moving out of my way.

"You're going to have to forgive Neuman and Lawson, and ..." She shrugged with amusement. "I guess, me. There's a tradition within the unit for new members, and if you're going be part of the team, you're expected to follow the tradition."

"And what's the...that, ma'am?"

"Oh, you'll see." And before I realized what was happening, the two men grabbed me and hauled me up onto their shoulders. "Enjoy yourself, Dodgson!" The Major called after me as they headed down the corridor. I couldn't help but laugh as I sat upon their shoulders and had to duck frequently to avoid the low-hanging beams of the Chesty's corridors. A couple of times, they even hit me against it. They found it quite amusing when I cried out and grabbed my forehead. I had no idea where we were going, and I was surprised when they took me down to the cargo hold.

As we entered, they started chanting, "Dodgson, Dodgson, Dodgson." I was surprised to see the room full of the Marines that had been down on Phobos. At least the ones that had survived to return. They took up the cry of my name. Clapping slowly in time with every time it was said. The group quickly parted, and I saw a chair set into a reclining position. My two escorts turned around so my back was to it, and they unceremoniously dropped me back and let me fall into it. It winded me for a moment. I have to admit that I got somewhat nervous as the group, still chanting my name, started to crowd around me, still clapping their hands. A woman I had not seen before in her thirties, possibly late twenties, stepped out of the crowd carrying a small spherical device. She raised her hand in the air, and everyone fell silent.

"Hi Dodgson, I'm Abigail Thompson, and as the oldest member of the squad...." She paused, grinned widely, and said with a shrug and a chuckle, "Well, apart from Jenna Plural, that is." And around her, everyone laughed. I didn't understand the joke because this woman was clearly older than Jenna Plural, from what I could see. "I have a singular privilege of inducting new team members." She continued. "Take your shirt off, Dodgson."

The smile on my face since I'd left Jenna's office suddenly evaporated. "What? W...Why?" I found myself saying, most bemused.

Still grinning, Thompson rolled her eyes. "It appears our new recruit requires some help, gentlemen." She said to Neuman and Lawson, who stood by either side of me, and again before I knew it, they grabbed hold of me, and my shirt was pulled over my head until I was sitting in that chair and just my military-issue bra.

"Holy fuck! She's seen some combat," someone muttered, but got a punch in her arm from a neighbor. I felt the eyes all around me boring into the crisscrossed line of scars about my shoulders.

"It's time to receive the Mark of Jenna," Thompson said and stepped over, holding the small ball over me. My eyes widened as I saw the top of it swivel open, and a large needle came out of it. Only then did I realize it was an automated tattoo gun. You simply programmed it with a design, and it burned into your skin.

"A tattoo?" I said as if it was the worst thing ever, but that only caused the group around me to laugh.

"Yes, Dodgson, we all have it."

And without a care in the world, she lifted her shirt above her breast and revealed the monochrome tattoo of the skull etched into her chest, surrounded by an intricate pattern going out to her shoulders and down the top of her breast. It was not something that I would ever have considered, but as she let go of the ball and it floated down towards me, not only did I realize I'd have no choice if I was to accept this honor from the Major, but I actually kind of welcomed it. My father would have been horrified, for it was against our faith to mark our bodies. A thought I wish he'd considered when giving me those scars.

I closed my eyes as the needle approached me, hoping it wouldn't hurt to a degree where I'd cry out and embarrass myself in front of all these people. As the needle went in, I couldn't help but wince, and the cries of 'Dodgson, Dodgson' went up again as the needle went in and out across my body rapidly. Apart from a slight burning sensation, it wasn't as bad as I'd expected, and it drew out the intricate pattern across my body. It took surprisingly little time, and just a few minutes later, I looked down at my red raw skin as the ball raised up, and Thompson took it once more. Lawson tossed me back my shirt, and I pulled it back over my head, and Neuman reached out his hand to help me out to the difficult position the lounging chair placed me in.

I was then led over to where there were cases of beer and one exceptionally large can. Neuman picked that one up and tossed it to me.

"You need to down it in one go, or it brings us bad luck for a year," Lawson said, and at first, I thought he was joking, but clearly, they took this superstition quite seriously. I'm not exactly a heavy drinker, so I was quite nervous as I broke open the can and everyone started shouting 'Go! Go! Go!' in a similar way they had shouted my name as I chugged on it. I was about halfway through when I started to choke, but as I instinctively made to bring the can down, Lawson's hand came up and held it in place. Beer splattered all over my face, but I did manage to get most of it down. Everyone appeared to find it acceptable, and they cheered when I crushed the can and tossed it onto the table. This was clearly a sign for everyone to help themselves, and I spent a most pleasant evening with some of the greatest Americans you could ever meet.

Unfortunately, I didn't carry such things as Alcorin pills that could offset the effects of alcohol, and Thompson had to help get me back to my quarters that night, which apparently amused her greatly. When I woke up for my first day working with Michael Phelkar, I had my first ever hangover. It was truly unpleasant.

I transferred over to the Lady Liberty and enjoyed the brighter décor and a room that had a bed, not a bunk. Quite a luxury. Working as a clerical assistant would not have been my first choice of position, but I wasn't lying when I referred to Phelkar as a very nice man. Whilst I admit working for a foreigner was usually a problem for me, he made it so easy.

His job was virtually the same as a First Officer in all but name. He was responsible for working out supplies, crew rosters, and enforcing the orders of the Major. The only way he differed from the first officer was that he couldn't give orders to anyone that hadn't specifically been assigned to work under him. Even then, technically, the orders were that of Jenna Plural, being relayed through him.

It kept me busy, and Mr. Phelkar was an absolute delight to work for. He was very kind and considerate and always took time out to check in on me. It was nice to have someone make a fuss about me and care about how I was doing.

Slowly, the news spread that Major Plural had arranged a rendezvous with all the other ships of the American fleet that had rejected the treasonous president's surrender. It was all getting rather exciting. Although, I was concerned about the rumblings that Major Plural would not be allowed to assume authority.

However, she didn't seem too concerned, and in a morale-boosting gesture, she arranged a celebration for all the crew of all ranks, and not just us members of her elite Theta Squad. And it was down to Mr. Phelkar and me to arrange everything. Of course, Mr. Phelkar had no concept of Marine tradition, so everything was left to me. I was well-versed in Marine traditions, so setting up everything was very straightforward. The Peons had quite a stash of booze on the Liberty, and I took advantage of it.

The party kicked off the next day at eight. The Liberty's officer's mess pounded to the music of the latest hits from the USA just prior to the capitulation. The first person I saw was Stacey Grant, and, of course, the raving alcoholic had taken over serving at the bar. As one would expect, she was dressed like a whore in a sleeveless white blouse and a ludicrously short, pleated tartan skirt. It was embarrassing, to say the least.

Helen Tracker was dressed appropriately in bell-bottom grey slacks and a matching button-up vest. All around were the elite of the USA in the best party gear they could keep in their footlocker. Dancing, drinking, and acting like war was a word they had never heard of.

Suddenly the music stopped, and all looked around, wondering why. A large beer keg rolled into the room, followed by another. A cheer went up. I noticed Mr. Phelkar looked confused, so I went over to him.

"It's the Marine tradition, Sir. Ever since the first Marines were sent into space. Just watch."

And as if on cue, Major Plural stepped into the room. Mr. Phelkar looked like his eyes were going to pop out of his head. I started to think that he had a thing for Major Plural. I couldn't blame him, because I certainly did. She was a goddess. She wore a tight black skirt just above the knee with a matching, almost translucent, sheer collared shirt. Her hair was tied back in a ponytail with a white scrunchie, and a gold chain with a locket hung down over her breast. She sported a pair of three-inch pumps with black stockings and a gold anklet on one ankle. Upon seeing her, we all stopped what we were doing, stood at attention, and saluted.

Major Plural stopped at attention at the entrance and returned the salute. Then the familiar tune of the Marine Hymn began to play, and all but a few army and navy personnel began to sing.

"From the Halls of Montezuma to the shores of Tripoli. We fight our country's battles in the air, on land, and sea."

The Star-Spangled Banner immediately followed this. All the while, no-one moved from their rigid spot at full attention. Then silence fell, and I watched Major Plural waiting for something to happen. She then lowered her head, everyone followed suit, and Grant began to sing. Some crap about Australia being great. Bleugh!

When she concluded, the attention returned to Major Plural.

"Boys and girls of the free United States elite forces. As your commander, I ask nothing less than your best. On Phobos, you gave me nothing less than your best. So, the beer is on me."

It was only then that I saw she carried a snap pistol behind her back. Raising it, she fired once into each keg, and a cheer went up, and Marines grabbed up their mugs to get what was called "The Commander's Fill," as it gushed over the floor.

Again as tradition would have it, we had to drink our first tankard in one go, each taking it in turns as the others shouted to us, 'Go! Go! Go!' Covered in beer, I grinned at Lawson as he asked me to dance, and I obliged. As we did, I looked over to where I saw Mr. Phelkar talking to

Stacey Grant. I so hoped that he wasn't getting involved with that Australian. She may have been on the side of the Americans, but she was uncouth and still a foreigner. Of course, I know Mr. Phelkar was also a foreigner, but there was something...different about him, and we had that Anglo-American 'special relationship' with the Brits. And I admit I wondered what it would be like to have my own 'special relationship' with the sexy accented Brit. It was like he was one of us. Grant, however, was like a fungus that clung to the dark side of the great oak that was the United States of America. An unrepentant drunkard from a culture so uncivilized they even ate their national animal, the kangaroo.

I wasn't aware of how much I was staring at them until I caught Stacey's eye, and grinning, she said something to Mr. Phelkar, who turned around and looked at me too. I got embarrassed, and I think I blushed slightly and turned away. At least, that's how Mr. Phelkar says I responded. I don't really recall.

However, parties do not mean duty can be neglected, and each of us enlisted personnel had to leave the party to patrol the ship or stand watch on the ship's defense monitors. Thompson slipped me an Alcorin pill to sober up as I left.

The ship seemed empty as I strode the corridors, with everyone at the party. However, toward the end of my hour, I heard a voice. A familiar one, and as I walked around the corner, I was startled to see Major Plural standing outside Mr. Phelkar's quarters. She had her heels off, held them in her hand, and was looking at him most provocatively, as he stood in his doorway conversing with her. Then she went inside, and the door shut. I didn't know what to make of this at first. Somehow I thought Major Plural would be above such things as relationships. But it wasn't my place to ever question her. A pang of extreme jealousy ran through me. However, the most frustrating part of that was I realized I was jealous of him, not her.

I had the option to return to the party when I was relieved of duty, but I chose not to and returned to my quarters.

Chapter Eleven

The Passion of Jenna

M r. Phelkar is probably the sweetest man I had ever met. He's strong and commanding, and that accent was just so dreamy. I can't deny I had more than a crush on the British diplomat. You would think that having become aware that he was now in a relationship with Major Plural, I would have lost interest, but honestly, that only made him more exciting. In a way, touching him was like touching her. He had seen her naked. He had touched her. He had intimately explored that perfect body. It'd sent tingles through my nether regions just thinking about it.

Working for him was amazing. He literally let me do everything and never questioned how I did it. He had taken over the second officer's quarters on the Liberty, and it had several rooms, one of which he converted to an office. That was where I worked. I hardly ever saw him though, and I'm sure he had other pressing matters to deal with. Occasionally, he would appear and check I had done everything I needed to before I headed 'home' for the night. However, I could go days without seeing him.

One such night, I had been alone most of the day and was working late, filling in reports, when he returned to his cabin. He looked tired and stressed as I looked up at him from my computer console.

"Oh, you're still here?" He muttered softly as he walked over to the drinks cabinet and took out a bottle of whiskey. "You really should get along and get some rest."

I smiled up at him. "It's all good, Sir. I enjoy what I do."

He looked at me as he stepped over to his small bar and poured a drink, then indicated the glass. "Would you like one?"

"No, thank you, Sir," I said. "I'm about to head off."

He smiled and sat in the armchair, which was the only furniture in the room, besides my desk. As he took a sip and swirled the drink in his hand, he studied me carefully. "You're a very attractive young lady, Corporal Dodgson. Did you know that?"

I smiled back, albeit a little uncomfortably. He was my boss, after all, and although he lived here, to me, it was my workplace.

I felt myself color up, and my heart went all a pitter-patter as it once had for Calvin Butler and thoughts of how he would say that to me.

"Come and sit over here and take a break," he patted the seat next to him.

Slowly I rose, and although a little unsure, I took my seat next to him. As I did so, my heart beat faster, and the idea he was hitting on me was quite intoxicating. However, maybe he was just being fatherly. Now that did make me uncomfortable, considering how my own father had treated me.

I sat upright with my knees together and my hands on my lap. He chuckled lightly.

"Relax, Dodgson." He said softly, and to my surprise, he placed a hand on my back and rubbed it gently. It felt so good. I looked across at him and smiled softly. The hand that touched Jenna was now touching me.

My lack of resistance appeared to cause his smile to widen, and he moved his hand down to rest upon my knee. We sat there silently as he tentatively ran his hand up and down my leg. Slowly but surely, he gradually moved it to the inner part of my thigh. I knew instantly that I should object, but the words wouldn't come. Then, he leaned in and kissed me. It was soft and gentle, and loving. Despite my better judgment, I gave in to it, but as I closed my eyes, I pictured Jenna in my head. His intimate knowledge of the woman who was both my hero...and my desire. To be with him would be like being with her. His hand slid between my legs, and I stiffened as my conscience battled momentarily between pleasure and responsibility. I found my breathing getting heavier, and my body tingled with tiny pinpricks. I should've said no. I knew that we should stop, but I found myself filled with the desire to know what he had done with Jenna. But I didn't know what to do. I didn't know where to put my hands, and I felt a little unsure as he kissed me again, and his tongue entered my mouth, the whiskey warm on his breath.

I'd never kissed Calvin like that, and it was uncomfortable yet pleasurable at the same time. My breasts heaved up and down with my heavy pants. He grinned at me as he pulled up my Marine-issue pullover, and I raised my hands to help him. I felt myself color slightly, as he threw the jumper aside and stared down at my breasts encased in nothing but my bra. I looked up at him longingly as he placed his hands on them. He then stood up and, taking my hand in his, pulled me up and against him, his other arm around my waist and pulling me against his body. As his mouth found mine again, I closed my eyes, but they quickly shot open again as I felt his hand unfasten the back of my bra and release it.

"Mr. Phelkar, we shouldn't do this," I murmured, melting into him as his lips caressed my neck.

"Hush!" He said softly as he slid the garment off me and tossed it casually aside. "It's okay. I promise you that you're going to enjoy this."

He leaned in to kiss me again. I was lost. I tentatively tried putting my tongue into his mouth, but it just felt too weird, and I was so uncertain, not knowing what I should be doing.

He stepped back and pulled his shirt off before pulling me back again, and my flesh touched his. The body against me that had pressed against Jenna. Oh my! I wanted to push him away again and make him stay loyal to the woman I loved, but the sensations coursing through my body were stronger than my resolve.

As his hands explored me, they finally slipped down to unfasten my belt, and, thinking I should do the same, I started to undo his. As he slipped out of his pants and I mine, I looked down at his exposed manhood that stood erect and jutted appreciatively in my direction. It was grotesque and disgusting and went some way to curb my ardor. I closed my eyes, not wanting to lose this wonderful sensation, and thoughts of Major Plural entered my head once more. Brave, confident Jenna Plural, and I found my aversion disappearing.

As his hands slid down to caress my thighs and ass, I imagined it was her touching me. He lifted me, and instinctively I wrapped my arms and legs around him, his hot member pressing against my belly as he carried me over to the bed in the corner of the room. My eyes were still squeezed tightly shut.

I could only see *her* face and feel *her* hands and body against me. Jenna Plural. I know you won't believe me, and some'll say I'm crazy, but I was now with Jenna. I don't know how she did it, but she replaced Mr. Phelkar as she gently lowered me onto the bed. Her long brown hair brushed against the sides of my face as her body came down on top of me. Then, slowly, sensuously, she violated my innermost sanctum. As my leader and the savior of humanity, this was *her* right to take me and use me in whatever way she pleased. I was hers.

I gave myself to her as a sacrificial offering, and while it hurt at first, enough to make me gasp in pain, it quickly passed, and the ultimate sensation of pleasure washed over me. I heard her grunt with pleasure, as she continued to work her way up to a crescendo.

"You're a good girl, Emma," I heard her say, but I still didn't open my eyes as she finished huffing and panting. However, I was disappointed, as I'd always heard that the woman was supposed to experience some ultimate plea-sure at the end of it all as well. As Jenna withdrew, I felt her flop down beside me.

I opened my eyes, and beside me, once more, she was Mr. Phelkar, and he lay there staring up at the ceiling, breathing heavily. I turned away and lay on my side, bring-ing my knees up to hug them. I ached, and the feeling of guilt flowed through me. I closed my eyes again, and I eventually fell asleep. When I awoke, I was alone in the room. I sat up, looking around the room before fumbling for my clothes. I dressed as quickly as possible and headed back to my quarters. We never spoke about it again and continued working together like it'd never happened.

The journey to the rendezvous in deep space would take several weeks. After Mr. Phelkar took her my calculations of the severe impact that it would have on our resources, Major Plural decided to upload most of the crew. She only kept two Marines downloaded; fortunately, one was me. This severely reduced my workload and meant I only went to work for about two hours a day. I spent a lot of my time watching very old 24th-century movies set in the early days of solar colonialism. I admit, I had a penchant for gushy old romance stories from those early days. I would lie in my bed with a big bowl of popcorn and a hot cup of cocoa and cry my eyes out over a corny love story.

Dozens of ships from all allied nations, except the Japanese, were coming together, and in the weeks that fol-lowed, that would become hundreds and include civilian vessels which, although uninvited, appeared to be wel-come all the same.

I don't know why I had assumed that Major Plural would arrive in a blaze of glory and be hailed as the free American people's new leader. I shouldn't have been surprised as I was when I heard her leadership was actually challenged. I was absolutely livid.

Although, of course, I never expressed it to anyone. I was just delighted that she chose me as part of her guard to attend a summit of captains on the U.S.S. Los Angeles.

I wore my dress uniform again for the first time since graduation. I felt proud as we waited to dock alongside the ship. Hardy and I walked directly behind her, and even Mr. Phelkar had to walk behind us until we were met by Captain Addison, commander of the Los Angeles and, if my opinion is worth anything, another sterling patriot.

The vessel was a top-of-the-line cruiser. We were led into a large briefing room where Major Plural took her place at the head of the table. She was wired up to a virtual reality device that would connect her to all the captains in the fleet while the rest of us watched on an overhead screen. The debate went on for a couple of hours.

There were some dissenters, and I made a mental note of their names and burned the recognition of their faces into my mind. This was where we separated grown-ups from the children. Finally, Major Plural was asked to leave while the captains discussed which way they were going to go. The absolute *audacity*.

As the major strode out, Hardy and I fell in behind her. An eternal wait began with Major Plural pacing back and forth, but I knew what the result would be, and yes, the vast majority backed her. Only a cowardly piece of slime wouldn't devote itself to the savior of humanity.

Then the Constitution arrived. The great experiment. A vast behemoth of a ship fresh out of the dock just weeks before the surrender. It was commanded by a piece of shit called Admiral Baines, and he refused to recognize Major Plural's authority. It seemed like it was game over for our side. We couldn't take out his ship without a massive loss of vessels and personnel.

However, this was not the end of it. I was summoned to a mission briefing with Major Plural, Addison, Tracker, and Hardy. I was punctual, but also the last to arrive. They were standing over a large table with plans of the U.S.S. Constitution laid out.

Major Plural glanced up at me as I entered the room. "Oh good, you're here. Grab yourself a coffee over there, and come and join us."

I didn't particularly want a coffee, but I took it as an order, poured myself one, and went to stand behind Hardy.

"Come around this side. You'll see better," Addison told me, and I went around. To my surprise, Addison stepped aside, leaving me a space between her and Major Plural. My heart pounded being so close to her. It is an experience I recommend to any patriot that has the opportunity.

"So, here's the situation," Major Plural continued. "We need to get Helen Tracker on board the Constitution without detection so she can disable the computer systems. Stacey's shown us that there is a blind spot just here." Major Plural pointed to a rear airlock on the plans with a long well-manicured finger that I so desperately wanted to touch. "We'll need Dodgson and Hardy to spacewalk her over there. When aboard, they're to get her to the central computer room...Here." The long perfect finger traveled across the floor plans to the room deep within the bowels of the ship. "You shouldn't need to fight your way through, as we'll have you dressed in the uniforms of techs serving aboard the Constitution. When Tracker has completed her business, you will remain there and protect her until we manage to board the ship ourselves. If successful, all power on board the ship will be out, so you'll need to gear up for night vision combat. Once we've taken the bridge, the pair of you will escort Helen to us. Pretty simple, huh?"

"Yes, Ma'am," I replied proudly, but Hardy sneered at me.

"I sent these floor plans to your personal devices and room computers. Get familiar with this layout. You need to know it better than you do your own ship," Addison advised us firmly. "The ship is vast and much bigger than it appears to be just looking at these plans. You can easily get lost if you don't know where you're going."

"Yes, Ma'am," Hardy responded, and I returned the sneer at him. Yes, all kinda childish now I think of it.

I went ahead of Hardy as we were dismissed, but he came up behind me.

"Hey, Dobson, wait up!" He said aggressively, and I turned to face him. "You should know that I strongly objected to a dumb rookie like you being on this mission."

I was on a high from being in the presence of our leader, and I wasn't going to let this big ox berate me. "Of course, that's your p...prerogative, Sergeant."

"Don't be funny, Corporal."

I hadn't intended to be. I thought I had come across as more flippant than whimsical.

"I don't know what you did to get all chummy with her, but it's my reputation on the line. I am this close to getting with her." He held his thumb and forefinger close together. "No goddamn rookie is gonna mess that up for me."

My high quickly deflated. How *dare* he speak of Major Plural in such a manner, especially as she was in a relationship with Mr. Phelkar and me?

"With all d...due respect, Sarge. I don't believe that someone like the Major would be seen d...dead with the likes of you, but then I can't imagine any woman wanting to be."

He sneered contemptuously at me. "You don't know what you're talking about. You didn't see us at that party."

"No, I had better things t...to look at. But, I did see the Major after the party, and she certainly wasn't w...w...with you," I said contemptuously. "She was with Mr. Phelkar, a man m...more suited to her st...station."

Rather than get offended, Hardy laughed.

"Then you must be the only one that doesn't know that the British shit is fucking Stacey Grant."

At that thought, I felt a small amount of vomit rise up into my throat and descend again.

"Mr. Phelkar wouldn't be so d...demeaning to himself to be seen with the likes of Lieutenant Grant."

Hardy screwed his face up in disgust at me. "You are such a weirdo, Dobson. Stacey Grant is no Jenna Plural, but she's still a nice piece of ass. I think you have some sort of screw loose."

At that, I replied, "Well, sh...she's certainly more in your c...c...class, Sergeant. But make sure you check in with the c...clinic after making out with her."

He shook his head at me. "Watch yourself, Dobson! Because I'll be watching you, and I'll make sure you're on report if you so much as move your pinky finger in the wrong way on this mission."

"Oh, I'll show you, Sergeant H...Hardy. I watch every-thing." As he turned away and headed down the cor-ridor, I shouted, "And the name is Dodgson, *Dodgson, D...D...*DODGSON!"

Without looking back, he waved his middle finger at me. "Whatever, Der Der Dodgson!"

Hardy! What an uncouth bully and so unbecoming of a Marine to have impure thoughts about our leader. I would have to deal with him at some point and...well...you know how I deal with bullies already, don't you?

CHAPTER TWELVE

KENSETT

A few days later, a woman called Charlotte Kensett left a message saying she wanted to meet with me. No rank or title was given, and it was rather curious. I'm not sure how I would have responded under different circumstances; however, she informed me that she was contacting me under the authority of Major Plural, and I took her word on that. I called back over to her office on the U.S.S. Los Angeles, and I made an appointment for that afternoon.

When I went over there, it was all rather strange. Her offices had a number on the door but no indication of its purpose, such as a department name. I entered, and again it was odd for her office was pristine and depersonalized. Her assistant greeted me pleasantly and showed me to her office in the back.

Charlotte Kensett rose from her desk and greeted me. She was dressed in civilian clothes – a black colored shirt with a full black skirt to match. She was possibly around thirty. Despite not holding a military title rank or uniform, she bore herself in a very military fashion, standing quite upright as she rose to greet me.

"Thank you for coming to see me at such short notice, Corporal Dodgson. Please take a seat." Saying nothing, I took the proffered chair. She returned to her own and sat back. "I've been asked by the Major to set up a new internal service to ensure security in the new situation we find ourselves in. Prior to this, I served as an agent for the Department of Outland Security."

I was impressed as Outland Security was a combined CIA, FBI, and Homeland Security division for all American off-world interests. American heroes in a clandestine world. However, something bothered me.

"You d...don't sound American," I said coldly. Her accent was distinctly upper-class British.

A thin smile crossed her bright red lips. "Oh, I can assure you I am an American. Would you like to see my certificate of naturalization?"

The offer, I'm sure, was not a serious one.

"That seems unnecessary, as Major P...P...Plural vouches for you," I replied.

"I'm glad that I have your approval, Corporal." She chuckled and sat back, studying me carefully. "Part of my responsibility is to assess everyone with regular access to her."

"That makes sense," I said. "There are m...many people who do n...not share her vision."

"Well, I'm glad I have your understanding." She picked up a pair of large, black-framed glasses and, putting them on, glanced down at her screen and then back up at me.

"I see there was an incident during your basic training. A recruit was murdered, and you were a suspect." She looked up at me again with a questioning look.

"Everyone was," I replied casually.

"Hmm, well, you were a little higher on that list than most. How do you explain that?"

"I was higher on the list because R...R...Randall and I didn't get along."

Her eyes narrowed as she removed the glasses and leaned her elbows on her desk. "You don't sound too upset about the death of one of your fellow colleagues in this manner."

"I'm not p...particularly," I shrugged. "He was a d...d...disgrace as a M...Marine and a disgrace of a human being."

Kensett looked a little surprised by my response. "That is quite an unusual admission by a murder suspect. Usually, people would try to distance themselves from any disagreements they've had with the victim."

"Isn't it more suspicious to b...be dishonest? Randall was a p...p...pig. Should never have worn the uniform," I said, a little annoyed.

"Strong words." Her cold smile returned. "I take it you are a patriot, Corporal Dodgson?"

"And with all d...d...due respect, I consider it an insult even to be asked that question," I said curtly.

She shrugged that off. "My apologies. It is simply part of my job."

"Your j...job, as I understand it is to r...root out undesirable elements within the m...military and government, not cast aspersions upon d...dedicated members of the United States Marine Corps."

She tilted her head quizzically. "Undesirable elements? Why don't you simply use the word traitor?"

"They are not n....necessarily the same thing. A person is only a t...traitor after they have committed treason. Is it not b...best to remove a problem before it becomes a p...problem, Miss K...Kensett?"

Kensett now stared at me in deep concentration, and instead of answering my question, she said softly, "Please do go on, Corporal Dodgson."

"Well, it is r...rather too late to do anything after the act of t...treason has been p...performed. We need to eliminate these th...threats before they become threats."

"What about their rights and due process?" She raised an eyebrow.

I stared at her. I couldn't help but wonder if she was the right person for intelligence. I found myself getting quite angry. "Rights are for the innocent. Rights were never intended for traitors, d...despite what the liberals say."

"Really? So, what should we do if we find these...undesirables?" She asked.

My suspicions about her intentions were heightened, but I spat the words out at her in my agitation.

"Eliminate them, Miss Kensett!" I banged my fist on the table, yet she didn't flinch. I was sure a slight smile was hidden amid those otherwise impassive features.

"Without a trial?" She chuckled and sat back, crossing her arms.

I stood up. "Forgive me, but I think this meeting is done. I don't know where you are going with this, and I no longer wish to participate."

"Emma!" She stood up, raising her hands defensively. "Do you mind me calling you Emma?"

I shrugged. "It's my name, and you are a civilian, so call me what you like."

She indicated the seat again. "Please sit back down, Emma. Just indulge me. But don't worry, whatever you say won't get you into trouble. To be honest, so far, I'm quite impressed."

I hesitated but eventually did as she asked, and we sat again. "Trials complicate things. All you end up with is some unpatriotic liberal lawyer coming along and talking about issues they had with their mommy and getting them acquitted," I blurted out in one breath.

Charlotte laughed at that, something I would find out that she rarely ever did. "So what do you propose we do with them?" She smirked. Was she making fun of me?

"I feel like you're trying to manipulate me now, Miss Kensett. You know what is supposed to happen to these people. Why do you need me to say it?"

Kensett just sat staring at me until it became uncomfortable. "Call me Charlotte." She said, and another long silence passed until I made to stand up again, and she said quite calmly and seriously, "How is it your stammer disappears when you get annoyed?

I was taken by surprise at the question and calmly replied. "I d...don't know. Why?"

"Well, according to your medical records, it's due to some form of irreparable brain damage."

"S...so?

"If that was the case, then you would have the issue whatever your mood."

"Are you here to assess my loyalty, or do you also have a doctorate in medicine?" I retorted aggressively.

Kensett paused before smiling again. "Quite right. I think we can work together, Emma. You and I."

I scoffed at this. "I think, Miss K...Kensett, you're p...playing with me. I graduated at the b...bottom of my year. B...barely. I'm not stupid, but I'm not the stuff of the c...c...cloak-and-dagger world, and you know it. I'm a Marine, and I'm keeping it semper fi."

"Oh, I have no intention of asking you to step down from the Marine Corps." She stated firmly. "But I believe you have the potential to represent the interests of Jenna Plural on another level."

Now that piqued my interest. "Do g...go on?" I said, returning to my seat.

"Let me give you a scenario. You were present at the summit of the fleet captains. You saw several of them oppose the leadership of Major Plural." She started to swivel slowly back and forth in her seat while toying with her glasses.

"Yeah," I replied irritably. "It was d...disgraceful. I understand they've b...been removed from office pending investigations of p...potential ties with the enemy."

Charlotte stared at me for a moment. She dropped her glasses and said, "There is no evidence of collusion. Their only action has been to disagree with Jenna Plural."

I could see her studying my reaction to that. I gave her none. At least not in my expression.

"Jenna P...Plural is our leader. I think anyone that stands in her way should b...be eliminated. It should be enough to be c....considered treason. It's all pretty simple. It's just there is no will to d...do what is necessary anymore."

"That's something Jenna intends to fix." I noted the informality with which she referred to the Major. "And that's why I am in this position. We have arrested these officers, but they haven't technically broken the law," she shrugged but kept her eyes fixed on my every reaction.

"Revolting against the rightful leader of our people isn't a crime?" I shook my head angrily. "If you're not willing to shoot them yourself, let me do it."

It was an off-the-cuff remark, but I meant it.

Charlotte smiled through her thin lips.

"Are you willing to prove that to me?"

"Miss Kensett, I met you for the f...first time less than thirty minutes ago. I d...don't believe I have anything to prove to you. My loyalty is to Major Plural and Major P...Plural alone."

"I'm trying to head up a team that will ensure the security of Major Plural. I answer to her and her alone, and she has given me a free hand to take whatever action is necessary to ensure the stability and security of her leadership. I want to make you part of that, unofficially."

"If this is aboveboard, w...why would you want to d...do it unofficially?" I scowled.

"You think Jenna Plural should soil her hands doing things that some fools will misinterpret or use in propaganda against her?" She said incredulously. "We must ensure the protection of those involved," she said it as if it should have been obvious to me. "Plausible deniability, Emma."

"If it serves the b...best interests of Major Plural, then, of course, I'm on b...board," I said, calming myself once more.

"There's only one thing holding me back here, Emma. I need more than your word. I need some evidence that you mean what you say. And as part of that, I'd like to know your opinion on what I should do with the dissenting captains."

"Well, it would be much ch...ch...cheaper to use four bullets than four t...trials, and we can g...guarantee the outcome," I said.

"And how would I explain their deaths?" Kensett tilted her head questioningly again.

I shrugged. "Isn't that what you're p...paid to come up with?"

"Indeed it is." Kensett smiled. "However, are you willing to show me that you are more than words?"

"If that is n....necessary." I shrugged again.

"Come with me." She then led me out of the office and took me down two levels to the bowels of the ship. It was a small cargo area that clearly wasn't being used for cargo. Several locked storage containers were there, and an ununiformed guard was standing outside. "Open one of them up," Kensett ordered.

The guard nodded and went to the nearest door. As he opened it, he shouted, "Move to the center of the room! Kneel down! Hands behind your head!"

"Thank you, Mr. Jones. May I have your snap pistol and nightstick, please?" Charlotte asked, and without question or hesitation, he unfastened both from his belt holster and handed them over to her, and she led me into the makeshift cell. A man, fairly elderly, judging by his grey balding hair, knelt in the center of the room facing away from us. "This is former Captain Armitage of the U.S.S. San Diego. He is one of the commanders who wants us to surrender to the enemy."

"The war is over." The commander said without turning around. "I just want to go home and see my family. My daughter graduates high school next month. We're tired of this war."

Charlotte smiled at me.

"It makes my job so much easier when they give me a confession of their guilt," she said conspiratorially, then offered me the snap pistol, and I looked down at it. "Go ahead. You're authorized to deal with the situation."

I frowned, but I took the offered firearm. "S...seriously?"

"Go ahead." She nodded toward the prisoner.

I raised the weapon and pointed it at the back of his head. I tried to squeeze the trigger, but I just couldn't do it. It made me feel sick. I looked at the gun. I looked at Kensett. "I c...can't do it."

Kensett looked most disappointed and gave a resigned sigh. "Fair enough, Emma. I thought we had something for a moment there. But it's all good." She reached out to take the gun from me.

I shook my head. "No, Charlotte, I d...don't think you understand." I turned to look at him with utter disgust. "I want to see his f...face. I want him to look at m...me when I do it. I want him to know what a p...patriot looks like. I want to be the last thing he sees. Just like M...Major Plural would."

"Oh my God, you're fucking insane!" The captain said and made to get up. Kensett swiftly swung the nightstick into the back of his legs, then across his shoulders, sending him back down with a cry of pain. She turned back to me, pushed her glasses back up her nose, and nodded.

"Get. Up!" I ordered, unable to hide the venom in my voice.

He didn't move, and Kensett stepped over to him again and poked him in the back of the head with the nightstick. "You heard the lady. Move!"

He struggled to his feet, knowing he was not permitted to remove his hands from the back of his head. He turned around to face me, and there was fear in his eyes, the fear only a cowardly un-American traitor would have. This was not a godly man, and I stared at him for a moment, enjoying the fact this traitor suffered God's wrath. I raised the weapon again, pointing it at his face.

"Please don't...My daughter." He implored.

"Maybe she'll g...grow into a fine young lady n...now that you'll no longer be an influence on her," I said softly and fired.

As his body fell to the floor, Charlotte turned to me with a wry smile.

"Welcome to the team, Emma." She put out a hand for me to return the gun to her.

"Yeah, yeah, but what about the other three?" I said impatiently.

"Oh, you don't need to worry about that. I just wanted to see that you were willing to do what it took."

"Oh, but I so w...wanted to." I sighed.

Charlotte raised an eyebrow. "I have another appointment soon. We'll have to be quick."

I had a euphoric feeling for the rest of the night. Four traitors sent to hell by my own hand. It felt so good.

Chapter Thirteen

The U.S.S. Constitution

The call came through that all was prepared for the assault on the U.S.S. Constitution. I was halfway through a really good movie. I can't remember what it was now, but I remember being very disappointed that I wouldn't see the end. At least, not that day. Hardy and Tracker were already there as I entered the bay where we were going to change into our EMU suits and get ready to crossover to the enemy vessel.

"You're late," Hardy growled at me.

I found this a rather curious statement. "No, I'm n... not, Sarge. A t...time wasn't specified other than to come now."

He muttered something under his breath, which I was sure was unpleasant as I saw Tracker give him a questioning frown.

Hardy had got the gear we needed ready. I pulled on the Constitution replica uniform and then the EMU suit over the top. I then slipped a snap pistol into the sleeve of the EMU suit, and I turned to Helen to check the connections on her back, and she did the same to me. When Hardy turned his back to me, I pretended not to notice, and he said, "Don't be childish, Dobson. Check my gear." I sighed and did as he ordered, pondering whether I should take this opportunity to loosen something, but the mission was more important, and he could wait.

"Do you two have a problem?" Tracker asked. "Because you're making me very nervous."

Hardy grunted in his usual manner, and I said, "No problem, Gunnery Sergeant. Sorry."

I have to say, despite his errant mouth, Hardy was good at what he did, and I trusted him as far as operations went. Not that that would ultimately redeem him from his inappropriate attention to Major Plural. No! Judgment was going to come for Mr. Hardy, eventually, but for now, all that mattered was getting Tracker to that computer room.

I could hear Helen breathing heavily over the internal communications, and I placed a hand upon her back to reassure her as the airlock slowly opened, and we looked out into the blanket of space. She seemed to breathe heavier as we saw the Constitution, a mere speck of light at this moment, shining in the vastness of the expanse we had to cross.

Tracker did not have a jetpack. She didn't need one and, even if she had, she didn't know how to use it. She'd never done a spacewalk before, and she wasn't even really doing one now, since Hardy and I clipped tethers between ourselves and her. Then, interlocking arms with her, we stepped out into the void, powering up our packs as we went.

The trip across was uneventful. For most of it, we were too small to be picked up on the ship scanners. However, as we drew close, we had to go in via a very narrow vector that Stacey Grant had laid out. It was the best way to avoid detection by going through the Constitution's blind spot. They didn't tell us prior to the mission about how outdated Grant's information was and the possibility of the flaw being fixed though. Telling us could have added unnecessary tension because we would've had to go anyway. However, her information proved solid, and we arrived at the assigned airlock several hours later, where we tethered ourselves to the fuselage and waited. Airlocks are not designed to be opened in space from the outside. It can only be done when a ship is in docking mode. This was to stop people from getting in during a battle. We just had to wait for whatever agents the Major and Kensett had arranged to aid us. A full ten minutes passed, and looking down at the air supply, I saw we were rapidly running out of time as the dial reached the halfway mark. Should it go over, there would be no way to return to the U.S.S. Los Angeles in time.

"Okay, that's it! Abort the mission." Hardy stated frustratedly.

"We can wait for a b...bit longer," I said.

"That's not your call, Marine." Hardy snapped.

"No, but it is mine," said Tracker firmly. "Everything rides on this mission. If we fail, we may as well turn ourselves over to the Peons."

"With all due respect, Gunnery Sergeant, I think that would be better than being dead," Hardy sneered.

If I had any doubts about the low levels that Hardy would sink to, I certainly didn't now. Dying for one's country is the noblest form of death, and I'm sure you can agree.

"I understand your concern, Sergeant Hardy, and I'm sorry, but we'll wait," Tracker said firmly. "The agents on the other side are personally handpicked by Charlotte Kensett, and trust me, I know exactly how good she is."

The only response from Hardy was an irritated sigh. A few minutes later, I looked down at my gauge again, and it was confirmed. Should we attempt to return to the Los Angeles, we would run out of air approximately seven minutes before arriving. I don't know anyone who could hold their breath for seven minutes. Our fate was sealed. We either entered the Constitution, or they picked up our corpses hanging outside.

When the airlock suddenly sank into the fuselage a few minutes later and slid aside, we all breathed a sigh of relief that we could still breathe a sigh of relief. We first pushed Helen in before detaching from the bulkhead and following her. The door closed behind us, and we detached ourselves from Helen as air filled the room and gravity was restored. We removed the EMU suits, which were then unceremoniously dumped on the floor. Then the internal door opened, and we stepped inside the Constitution. We never got to see the individual who had let us in. They had done it remotely from another location. Once the inner airlock closed behind us, we casually strolled down the corridor, chatting aimlessly, passing other crewmen who were unaware of our intentions.

We turned down the right corridors as if they were familiar, as Hardy and I had memorized the directions. When we crossed the threshold of the restricted area, we knew it wouldn't be that easy anymore. As we turned another corner, a crewman approached and asked us to show him our authorization for being in the area. Of course, we had no such documentation, so I stepped up to him and quickly pulled my snap pistol out of my belt as if reaching into my back pocket. I thrust into his stomach and fired, as Hardy stepped behind him and covered his mouth to avoid any potential screams or calls for help.

I admit that I do feel guilty for this particular demise, as I don't know whether he would have been loyal to Major Plural or not. It turned out that in the end, most of the crew were patriots. I re-holstered my weapon as the man expired. Hardy then lifted him over his shoulder and said, "Keep going. I'll find somewhere to stash this guy, so he won't be found for a while."

So alone, Tracker and I continued and eventually found the computer room. The security was simple. Someone was always present, and it could only be opened from the inside. That, of course, is if you don't have a Helen Tracker. She pulled out a device, slapped it on the lock, pressed a few buttons, and it made an irritating buzzing noise until it finally beeped, and the door slid open. I stepped in and shot the first startled tech in the face, then fired at the second. I cursed myself as I missed, giving them time to duck down behind a console. I went to fire again, but Tracker grabbed my arm.

"Careful you don't hit the computer."

I stepped around the counter where the last tech was crawling on the floor and put him out of his misery with another single shot. Tracker was already tapping the keyboard.

"Damn it to Hell!" Tracker exclaimed. "They've added an additional firewall that I didn't anticipate." Her fingers darted over the keyboard faster than I'd ever seen anyone type. "Every time it looks like I'm going to bring it down, the code rewrites itself and buries itself deeper into other code. It's actually quite beautiful, if I was on the other side of this."

I spun around as the door opened, aiming my gun. I lowered it just as quickly when I saw that it was Hardy. He turned around and reached out the door to grab Tracker's device to bring it inside before the door closed. Now we were in control of who could enter and exit.

"How is it going?" he asked.

"She's having p...problems," I said. "Something about c...code and stuff."

He turned to Tracker. "Can you do it or not?"

"Maybe, but it'd be easier if you shut up and leave me alone."

He turned away and muttered, "Dumb bitch," and even Tracker stopped what she was doing to look up and glare at him for a second.

"Okay, I'm in," she said, turning back to the console. "But I don't know how long I can hold back the algorithm for the firewall, 'cause it's rewriting its code again."

Hardy and I pulled on our night vision glasses as she started typing again. It was quite a eerie sensation as everything shut down. You get so used to the hum and vibration of a ship that you don't feel or hear it, but become instantly aware when it's no longer there. Slowly the ship died, and the lights went out last of all. Hardy and I switched on our emergency lights attached to our night vision glasses which we hadn't activated yet. Silhouetted in the dim light, Helen spoke to us.

"I don't know how long this is going to stay down for. It could come up at any time. This firewall is state-of-the-art. I'm gonna have to stay here and constantly monitor it."

"That's not part of the plan, Sergeant," Hardy said.

"There's no other option!" She snapped back at him.

"Yes, there is." He slipped a limpet mine from his belt, slapped it on the computer, and pressed the button before we could say anything. There was a fifteen-second delay, and we ran out the door and dove to the floor as it exploded. Tracker was positively livid as she rose to her feet.

"Hardy, you're a fucking dumbass. We're now never gonna get the ship online again."

With snap pistols out, we turned off the flashlights, turned on the night vision glasses, and slowly made our way toward the bridge. We started hearing the dull thuds on the outside walls. The sound of our troop pods launched from the Los Angeles, hitting the hull. Normally they would blow their way in, but we wanted the ship intact, so they began drilling.

It was over before it began. Americans were not going to easily kill other Americans without good cause. The Constitution crew started surrendering immediately as our troops swept over the ship. I would learn later that the

Major herself came on board and personally took command from Admiral Baines. He would officially announce his resignation, and we never heard from him again.

I became part of the emergency team, thanks to Hardy's screw-up. We had to set up emergency lighting in the ship's key areas, and Helen and her team managed to get some operational life support working.

As Helen predicted, she couldn't bring the system back online, and the ship was a dead weight hanging in space. That didn't stop us from taking control, and Helen worked through the night for several days to make the inside of the vessel functional.

Mr. Phelkar transferred over to the Constitution, as did most of the senior crew from the Lewis Puller. I eventually returned to aiding Mr. Phelkar and reviewed the records that had been sent to us of supplies and equipment. We had a stroke of luck. One of the US vessels had been transporting a computer system, similar to the Constitution, for an upgrade for another ship. As soon as I informed Helen Tracker, she commandeered it via Captain Addison. Major Plural officially transferred her command to the Constitution, and Addison came with her as her first officer. I worked closely with her, as she often liaised with Mr. Phelkar on supply and crew issues. Several days later, Tracker restored all of the internal power, but the engines and defense systems were still offline. It was announced that, henceforth, Jenna Plural was now Admiral of the Free Forces fleet. Rumors that the new Admiral was going to give officer commissions to all the members of Theta Squad to 'ensure there were people she could trust in significant positions' reached my ears, and I wasn't sure what to make of it. Me? An officer, just weeks – when you exclude M.E.T. oblivion – out of basic? I both wanted it and didn't want it at the same time.

When things started to develop some semblance of order, I actually got an evening off duty and ventured out to a mess hall. These were more like nightclubs and bars on this vast ship. The Constitution had been designed to go years without the need to dock, and as such, many of the comforts of civilian life had been included in its design.

As I entered the bar, I found Mr. Phelkar sitting alone on a comfy-looking couch, nursing a beer and deep in thought.

"Hey there, Mr. P...Phelkar." He looked startled as he looked up at me with those beautiful brown eyes. This quickly changed to his usual warm smile. "Mind if I j...join you?" I asked.

"I would be delighted by your company," he replied, sitting up and indicating the armchair chair opposite him.

"Th...thank you, Sir," I replied. As I sat down, he waved to one of the stewards.

"So, how are you doing?" He asked me with genuine concern.

"I'm okay," I shrugged.

"Is there something you want to talk to me about, Corporal?"

"Well, Sir, there's a rumor that Admiral Plural it's going to give me a commission. Make me an officer."

"Ah!" He smiled at me. "Well, I have not heard anything specifically about you, but I will say this. If Jenna Plural thinks you have what it takes, then you have what it takes."

"Yes, Sir," I replied, unconvinced.

"You know, I'm not an officer. You don't have to call me 'Sir.' You don't even have to call me Mr. Phelkar. My name is Michael."

"What sort of a name is Phelkar?" Stacey Grant suddenly appeared, jumped over the back of the couch, and landed next to him. He gave me an apologetic smile and rolled his eyes, clearly annoyed that she had interrupted our private moment. "I mean, it's not like it's even a real name."

"It was a tradition back when Martian independence was a thing," he advised. "People started making up names that had no national boundaries. My surname would have been Phillips, had my parents been born on Earth. That was before the war, and both sides decided that discussing independence for Mars was treason."

Stacey looked utterly bored as he spoke and very rudely yawned before looking at me. "Phelks is an okay bloke, but he can sometimes be such a long-winded wanker."

I tried to smile back. "Yes, Ma'am," I said curtly.

The stupid Australian didn't seem to pick up on the fact that Mr. Phelkar, nor I, wanted her here. "We're off duty. Cut the Ma'am shit and call me Stacey. Actually, cut the Ma'am shit altogether. I don't go in for that."

No respect for the chain of command. I did not find that surprising. Australians are not exactly cultured or well-educated. "Yes, ma... I mean St...St...Stacey."

"Seriously, Dodgson. Tonight, we leave the war behind us," she smiled, not that cheeky smile she perpetually wore, but a more sincere one.

I smiled coldly.

"Then please c...call me Emma." I said sarcastically.

Stacey grinned her stupid grin. "How 'bout I call you Em and make it more Aussie-like?"

Oh, my sweet God! She was as dumb as shit, but I just laughed it off. "As you wish."

"I've worked with you a while now, but I don't know much about you," Mr. Phelkar asked me. "Why did you join the Marines?"

"Bloody hell, Phelks," Stacey interrupted rudely. "You have two of the hottest women in the damn fleet sitting here, and you wanna talk shop!" She winked at me. I chuckled lightly, embarrassed for her.

Stacey ordered some shots for us before turning back to me. "So, how come a cute girl like you is all alone?"

"Well, I w....wasn't alone." I snapped back but flushed slightly when Mr. Phelkar winked at me seductively.

I know Mr. Phelkar never talked about our relationship in his book, but that just shows what a true gentleman he is. He knows we could never be together, for Major Plural had taken him as her own, and that was her right. However, I'm not ashamed of it, as you will see when I conclude this story, it was meant to be.

Stacey grinned and, without any semblance of manners, said, "I'm sorry. Did I interrupt something? You know, I always thought you preferred girls."

I was taken aback. Although it was only kind of true – I happened to like boys and girls equally. But I had done nothing to reveal that to this mouthy Aussie. "What have I ever d...d...done to give you that idea?"

She shrugged. "You remind me of a friend of mine. My best mate, actually. She liked the ladies."

Mr. Phelkar came to my rescue. He was such a darling man. "You must be worried about her with everything going on."

Stacey went on about some dead friend of hers, but I wasn't listening to her boring story, as the steward returned with our shots. I usually don't imbibe hard liquor, but the Australian slut had made me *so* mad.

"Same again, and keep them coming." Mr. Phelkar instructed as he took his.

"Nice one, let's call this a party." Stacey grinned.

Oh my gosh, that was it for me. "Actually, I should probably go," I said.

Stacey looked over at me, her expression softer. "I'm sorry, mate. I've made you uncomfortable. I didn't mean to. Please stay."

"Stacey's mouth is more active than her brain," Mr. Phelkar grinned at me but had that 'please don't leave me alone with this insane woman look upon his face,' and for his sake, I stayed.

"Ain't that the truth." Stacey smiled. "You're quite a cute girl," she said appreciatively.

Oh gross! However, the Melbourne Firebomb drink was going to my head fast, and I giggled.

"I'm *really* not into women," I lied, thinking she was about to hit on me. Oh, so vile!

Stacey shrugged. "Nor am I. At least, I wasn't until I met Jenna Plural. Now she *is* hot."

That was something we could agree on. "Now that, I cannot deny."

"You can't help but wonder what she's like in bed with all that genetic perfection," Stacey downed her third firebomb.

"I don't think that's an appropriate way to talk about our commanding officer," Mr. Phelkar said. Of course, he was absolutely right.

"More inappropriate than rooting her, Phelks?" Stacey grinned.

"What are you talking about?" Mr. Phelkar, again the perfect guy, jumped to the defense of Major Plural's honor.

Stacey grinned at him. "Rumor has it, that you're fucking the major."

"I don't know what you're talking about." He insisted.

"Looks like we're both outmatched when it comes to gaining the affection of Mr. Phelkar," the hussy said to me with a chuckle.

My head was swimming by now as I'd drunk my third shot, and I came to realize hard liquor had an effect on my speech too. "Well, it certainly increases the challenge." The firebombs were taking effect, and I found myself saying things I otherwise wouldn't.

"Well, he knows what he is missing with me," Stacey grinned, glancing up at me.

After downing another firebomb, I glared at Stacey. "Is there anyone that Mr. Phelkar isn't sleeping with?" I was again being sarcastic, but it went straight over her head.

"Well, it's not like he's an amazing stud or anything, but there was an amazing lack of men on the Chesty."

"Well, thank you," he snapped at her.

She just laughed. "Oh, come on, Phelks, I'm just joshing you, ya moron." She slipped her arm into his. "So, you and the boss. That's just a rumor?"

"Of course it is," he stated firmly.

Stacey looked over at me. "So, what do you think of a young Emma here? She's quite a cutie."

"She's younger than my daughter."

"I like older men," I replied without thinking, the liquor now having a hold over my filters.

Stacey glared at Mr. Phelkar. "How old do you think I am?"

"Never thought about it, to be honest. How old are you?"

"I'm twenty-seven." She then looked at me. "How old are you?"

"I'm nineteen."

He grinned and shrugged. "And my daughter is twenty-two, so I stand by my statement."

"You're such a fucking arsehole." Stacey pouted.

We drank some more, and I saw Mr. Phelkar staring at me invitingly. If he wanted me again, he could have me, and I let him know by returning the look. However, he said, "As nice as this has been, I think I'm going to retire. I have to be up early in the morning."

"You see, Em, that's the problem with older guys. They may know what they're doing in the bedroom, but have no stamina."

I laughed and found myself saying, "It's the knowing what they're doing that makes them most interesting."

"And on that note, I will bid you, ladies, goodnight."

"Yeah, yeah, fuck you, mate." Stacey grinned at me.

She watched Phelkar go with a look of deep concentration. She then looked back at me.

"Sorry mate, but I'm hornier than a jumbuck in the mating season, and I think he is too." She jumped out of her seat. "Catch you later, Em."

I watched her leave with disgust on my face. Surely Mr. Phelkar would not demean himself with that potentially pox-ridden woman?

They say that curiosity killed the cat, but I didn't care since I hate cats. As she reached the door, I got up and followed her from a discreet distance. She stopped outside Mr. Phelkar's cabin, and I had to duck around the corner as she turned back toward me. Fortunately, she didn't notice me. When I looked back around the corner, she was pacing up and down. She stopped and reached into her pocket, pulled out a small bottle of pills, popped one into her mouth, and then continued pacing again. A couple of minutes later, she knocked on the door. Mr. Phelkar opened it, and they stood talking for a moment, although I couldn't hear them. To my utter horror and disgust, he leaned in and kissed her quite passionately. Poor Mr. Phelkar. He made to pull her into the room, but instead, she pulled him out, and they turned in my direction. I disappeared back down the corridor and returned to the mess hall.

Some people would blame him for his part, but it wasn't his fault. Men are weak, and it's hard for them to resist the temptations of a woman. It's her responsibility to ensure she doesn't arouse him. If she does, she has to face the consequences and rectify the issue. Well...at least, that's what Papa always told me.

CHAPTER FOURTEEN

THE BATTLE OF DEEP SPACE

As I re-entered the mess, I headed straight toward the bar, and as I ordered my drink, I didn't realize that I was standing next to Helen Tracker until she spoke to me.

"Hey Em, how's it going?"

I turned and looked at her. I don't know if it was the drink, but she appeared more attractive than usual. Her flame-red hair hung around her shoulders rather than tied back as normal.

"Hey, Sarge. Well, it was going well...until that Australian showed up."

"Who, Stacey? She's pretty cool once you get to know her." She laughed. "But it's not easy to get to know her. Despite her behavior, she's pretty tight-lipped about herself."

I just harrumphed and paid for my beer. Tracker looked around, then back at me. "Well, you're alone, and I'm alone. You up for some company?" she asked.

I smiled at her. "Sure, why not?"

We found a quiet secluded corner and chatted away about anything but work. She told me about growing up in New York, and I told her about my life in Arizona, excluding the parts involving my father. We discovered a common passion for old movies, and when the barman called for last orders, she suggested we go back to her place and watch one.

The one difference between Helen and me, was that she was a lot messier than me. Not exactly dirty, just untidy. She seemed to bring work home with her, and pieces of old tech were lying around everywhere. The couple of chairs she had were piled high with chipboards and spare parts.

"Oh, don't worry about that. We can just sit on the bed." She laughed at the look on my face as I stared at the mess.

As I stared at her large widescreen television, I asked, "How come you have this and I don't?"

I pouted, since mine was tiny in comparison.

She looked a little embarrassed as she said, "Think of it as an engineer's indulgence. One of the first things I wired up was my TV. It's not considered an essential service, so I couldn't do it for everybody, but I'll see what I can do for you tomorrow."

She heated some nachos with melted cheese. Basic cooking facilities in our quarters were something we didn't have before coming to the Constitution.

She then jumped onto her bed, scooted over to the side by the wall, then patted the place beside her.

"Come on," she said, but I hesitated momentarily. "I'm not going to bite you. Well, not unless you ask me to."

I took the last statement as an innocent joke. I laughed lightly and climbed onto the bed beside her.

We didn't watch an old movie in the end. Instead, we put on a modern comedy that had come out just before the fall of the US. I couldn't help but wonder what had happened to the famous actors and actresses that were in the film, but it was funny, and we laughed a lot. Towards the end, with the nachos finished and the plate tossed aside, I felt Helen's hand upon mine, and looking down, I saw she was holding it. My eyes moved up to gaze into hers, and she was returning the look as she bit her lower lip. She moved towards me, and I leaned into her, and we kissed. Her hands caressed their way up my body, and I found myself pulling her closer, against me.

Helen was so tender and giving that it was like nothing I had experienced before. Her hands were soft and gentle, and her kisses were hard and passionate as we explored each other's bodies. The whole experience was just amazing. I eventually fell asleep in her arms, feeling secure for the first time in my life.

Just as I thought my life was becoming perfect... The fucking Peons attacked.

A vast armada was heading our way. Most of their damn fleet as it happened. They were going to throw almost everything at us as a final strike to wipe out the last opposition to their rule. The Battle of Deep Space was going to be a make-or-break event.

The pressure was on Helen to get the new computer up and running to bring the U.S.S. Constitution online. I was placed on the defensive line. My role was to join the team stopping anyone who managed to board the Constitution. It wouldn't be easy, considering we still had limited lighting, no internal defense systems and the ship couldn't move, making it easier for Peon troops to land on the outside and blow their way in. However, as was the nature of battle in space, there were never any surprises, and we could see who was coming from all directions. The Admiral had the option to get her faster ships out of there, but that would mean abandoning the Constitution and some of the civilian ships that had started to join the flotilla.

One of the things that someone of my rank found frustrating was not knowing the details of the battle plan. I was pissed when I heard that a group of ships under the command of Captain Addison had taken off. I had no idea this was part of the Admiral's plan, and I doubted my judgment of character, as I personally found Addison to be a sterling individual.

I was teamed up with Malcolm Hardy again. While I wasn't overly pleased with that, at least it was someone I knew how to work with. He may have been a pig of a man, but he was an efficient Marine. However, I was pleased to be issued the new Glock penetrators. They were an upgrade from our usual snap pistols, carrying a larger round at a much faster velocity. We were also issued Ruger P7 assault rifles, since the chance of a hull penetration on the Constitution was negligible. We were only to switch on our communicators to pick up status reports and orders. I couldn't even communicate with Hardy, and we would need to work with hand signals when silence was necessary.

We were near the bow of the ship when the attack came. Unbeknownst to me, the battle had raged for a couple of hours before anyone got near the Constitution. Admiral Plural had done everything she could to protect the flagship, her most powerful weapon. However, there was no doubt some would get through as this was a primary target, and it would be even more so once they discovered it just hung in space, not even able to launch the hundreds of fighters of the Air Force.

When the attack came, it was strange because we could barely hear the thud-thud-thud of troop capsules landing up on the outside. The hull was so thick with mercuranium. It absolutely tickled me when I later learned that the initial attempts to blast through backfired because they used insufficient explosives to get through the hull, and fireballs blew back into the capsules, killing those who had started the attack. How hilarious!

They quickly adapted and began manually burning their way through the bulkheads with torches. It wasn't a particularly productive move because we literally stood in front of where they were burning through and opened fire into the capsules as soon as they opened up. However, the sheer quantity thrown at us eventually became overwhelming, and Peons started getting through onto the ship.

It appeared at first that we would lose, as we started to be forced out of the outer corridors, losing many troops in the process. We kept up firing as more and more men filled the corridors. As more and more of our people started shouting, "I'm out," referring to their ammo, Hardy called for a retreat. We withdrew further into the ship, away from the bulkheads.

I don't know how many we killed that day. I was mowing them down with delight. Yet more were constantly coming in. I know the final count is estimated to be that they lost three times what we did.

Things started to seem lost until Helen managed to bring one of the defenses online and electrified the outer hull. Anyone who was outside the ship fried instantly, like bacon in a pan. It also meant no more troops could land. However, that didn't mean a certain victory, because should those already aboard take the bridge, they could disable Tracker's work or do what Hardy did and blow up the computer room again.

With Hardy and me out of ammo, we could do nothing but hunker down in one of the rooms and hope more supplies could reach us. We hid in some officer's cabin, and after radioing in our location and situation, we learned that the Los Angeles had managed to get more troops on board on the opposite side of the ship.

For us, though, the battle was over for the time being. We stood back, out of sight of the door, so we could hear if someone entered before they saw us.

I don't recall how the subject came up, but as we sat and talked, Hardy found himself saying, with considerable irritation, "I can't believe she's fucking that English loser."

"She is our leader," I shrugged. "Who she ch...chooses to make l...love with is entirely her own concern. She deserves whoever she ch...chooses to have."

Hardy looked at me and laughed. "Make love? You're a strange little bird, Dobson. Why on Earth Jenna made you a corporal, I'll never understand. You really don't have what it takes to be a Marine."

I was already annoyed at him, and this only aggravated me further. "Because I choose not to talk like some uneducated brute, that makes me less of a Marine?"

"Your sycophantic defense of that pathetic Englishman is what makes you less of a Marine, Dobson." He snorted.

"Mr. Phelkar is a gentleman and a fine man," I said with irritation.

"Not while he's fucking my girl. Something has to be done about him, and I promise you, little girl, I will remove him from the picture...somehow."

"I think it is disrespectful to speak about the Admiral that way." I was sure that I was reddening in my anger. "And she is not your girl."

He grinned.

"Not yet, Dobson, but she will be. I can promise you that." A filthy grin crossed his smug face. "And then I will part those sweet cheeks and have my way. Ooh, wee!" He laughed.

It took me a moment to realize he was not talking about her face, and that's when I decided it was now or never. Hidden in the fog of war, he would just be another casualty.

As Hardy turned away, I reached up behind him. I brought my arm around his throat and my knee into his back, pulling him toward me. It was foolish, for he simply used his superior weight and swung forward, throwing me over the top of his head with sheer brute force. I landed flat on the floor in front of him, and as I looked up, I was staring at the blade of his combat knife pointed directly at my face.

"What the fuck do you think you're doing, girl?"

"My duty, Sergeant." He was so confused that he wasn't paying that much attention. I swung my arm up, knocking the weapon aside, and with my other fist clenched tightly, I punched him right in the groin. He let out a cry and took a step back. It was just enough for me to get back on my feet. I swung a kick at his wrist, and he dropped the blade as I reached for my own knife attached to my thigh. Which I suppose, with hindsight, I should have used initially. Oh well!

He came at me, slamming me against the wall and winding me. My knee came up into his balls as I headbutted him. His grip loosened, and I tried to shove him back. But his forehead slammed into my face, my head snapped back to hit the wall hard, and blood flowed from my lip as my teeth cut into it. I believed at that point that I would not win this fight. All the tactics in the world didn't make up for the sheer brute force of a giant man against a skinny girl from Sedona.

He still looked bewildered by what was going on, but as I tried once more to withdraw my blade, he punched me again, and it fell to the floor with a clatter, as I hit the wall again. He moved to grab his knife off the floor, but as he leaned over, I slammed a knee into his stomach. It's kinda funny looking back at it now. It was almost a farce, as we both tried to snatch weapons, but to no avail. Alas, this time, I'd only hit his body armor, and he was barely fazed as he pulled up his rifle to strike me.

I tried desperately for a Hail Mary. Leaping into the air, I wrapped my arms around his neck and my legs around his waist, bringing him down with the sheer force of my forward momentum. He slammed down on the ground with me sitting on his chest. I knew I couldn't hold him for long, as his arms weren't pinned, and I punched, and I punched, and I punched the shit out of him. I hit him in the face every time he tried to push me off, and I resisted with sheer determination. I continued to pound his ugly face until it became a bloody pulp.

His body grew weaker under me, and his arms fell to his sides. I slipped my hands around the thickly muscled neck. It was so large I could barely get a grip around it, and he threw me back with a sudden burst of energy, and I landed on my ass between his legs.

He sat up, but I breathed a sigh of relief as I could see he was blinded by the blood in his eyes. I brought my knee up to my chest and slammed the heel of my boot into his groin. He rolled over in the fetal position, crying in agony. I got to my feet and looked around the room. Grabbing a bedside lamp, I yanked it out of the socket and placed it on the floor. I put my foot on it and pulled the cable out of its connections.

Hardy was trying to get up, so I gave him several hard whacks with the lamp across the side of the head until he lay groaning and barely moving. I tied the wire into a lasso. I placed it over his head and lifted him by the hair to get it around his neck. Dropping him, I then placed my foot on his head and pulled with all my might so that it tightened. He seemed to recover slightly once more and grabbed at his neck, unable to make a noise or even breathe. But I knew it was over for him then and there. I pulled harder, bent down, pulled his head up once more, and wrapped it several times around his neck as his struggles weakened. I tied the cord into a double knot and stood up to admire my handiwork. Not bad, but it didn't feel quite sufficient. No... I felt no satisfaction.

His knees were pulled up, and I gently slipped my boot between them to make them part, and they did so without resistance as I let him grasp at his throat, trying to undo the cable. I then slammed my heel into his testicles several times. In fact, I think I actually lost count. I didn't take the opportunity to check what damage I'd done, but I'm fairly certain that, should he have survived, his ardor for our leader would be seriously diminished. Or any woman, for that matter. It is a constant delight to me that men have these extremities that can give a woman incredible pleasure in more ways than one.

My attack on his precious jewels had the effect of creating his need to scream, but obviously, he couldn't, and it not only increased the pressure, but now... he was suffering. The body is such an amazing thing. You would be very surprised how hard it struggles to remain alive.

I stood watching in fascination and a little excitement as this servant of evil struggled to remove the cord. His face started to turn a nice shade of blue, like delphiniums in the summer. I was a little disappointed when his bulging, blood-stained eyes rolled up into his head, and he stopped moving. I sighed and got down on one knee to feel for a pulse. He was most definitely dead. However, I wanted to make absolutely sure. So I placed my foot upon his neck, grabbed his hair, and pulled hard until I heard the crack of his vertebrae.

I slumped into a chair to catch my breath. I laughed lightly, quite proud of myself. No-one was going to disrespect my leader. I then removed the cable from his neck and dropped it into the garbage chute to ensure my DNA was not present on the method of his death. Not that there was likely to be an autopsy. Malcolm Hardy would be just one of the many dead that day.

I carefully re-entered the corridor making sure it was clear. I had to put some distance between myself and Hardy's body.

Fortunately, the fighting had moved on, and it was relatively calm until suddenly, the ship shook and shuddered, and I seriously thought we were about to break up. I sat down and covered my head with my hands in the normal emergency procedure, but everything went calm except for the occasional thud against the hull.

I didn't know it at the time, but we had just got caught in the wake of the impact between the Lady Liberty as Stacey Grant took out a Peon cruiser with a head-on collision, and the dull thuds that followed were parts of those ships hitting us as they broke up.

I had no idea where I was, and as things settled, I looked up with trepidation before getting up again. I decided to continue heading on toward the bridge. I stopped when I heard German voices ahead of me, but I knew it was game over for the Peons when the mini guns dropped out of the ceiling.

I quickly checked to make sure I had the transponder pin this time. It was blinking away, letting the automated sensors know I wasn't a target. The distant sound of the machine guns firing showed me how far the enemy was from me. When they stopped firing, I continued on. When I arrived at the bridge, I saw Admiral Plural had boarded the ship during the combat, and my pride in her swelled. She had put herself in harm's way and didn't hide like many leaders when her people were fighting.

The bridge was a hub of activity, and as she stood on that bridge giving orders, the sun appeared on the screen. A distant shining globe, causing her to become a silhouette with a golden hue about her. I wish I could have captured that moment in a photograph, but it will be forever imprinted in my mind.

She looked at me with concern at my bloodied and bruised state.

"Are you okay?" She asked.

I nodded. "Was good to get some payback after what happened on the Chesty," I grinned.

The new Admiral gave me a wide smile. "Amen, sister," she said. "Now go wash up and get that face seen too, Corporal."

"Yes, Ma'am."

As I turned to leave, she asked, "Where's Sergeant Hardy?"

I looked back sadly. "I'm sorry, Admiral. He didn't make it. I..."

Admiral Plural sighed. "That's war for you, Corporal. Don't let it get to you, and don't forget it, either. Oh, and

163

by the way...change into a uniform more fitting to your new commission, Dodgson. I'm making you an officer. Lieutenant Dodgson."

I couldn't help but return her grin when she said that.

CHAPTER FIFTEEN

BIRTH OF THE CONFEDERATION

Although we took many casualties that day, victory was ours. We lost several ships, including the Lady Liberty and the Lewis Puller.

I was surprised when no one else ever asked anything about Malcolm Hardy. He appeared on casualty lists a few days later, and a few days after that, he appeared on the mass funeral ledgers as having been ejected into space. The time-honored tradition for the dead since man first ventured out amongst the stars. I was most sad to hear of the death of Neuman, but he died during the first assault on the Constitution defending Jenna, so I'm sure his wife and kids back home would be relieved to hear he died a hero.

Crews started receiving new orders as, once more, transfers were needed to fill vacant positions across the flotilla. I started to become concerned when I didn't receive my orders. It was like I'd been forgotten. I also didn't see Helen much these days, and I put it down to her being extremely busy, but when she never returned my calls, I started to get concerned.

I eventually received a call to visit with Captain Addison. Or rather, Commodore Addison now. I went to her office by the bridge. I was curious to see they were setting up television cameras in the center of the Constitution's vast control center. Apparently, there was going to be some sort of broadcast, but I quickly went in to see Admiral Plural's number two.

I was surprised to see her dressed in civilian clothes. It was the first thing she spoke to me about.

"Ah, Dodgson! Come on in and take a seat. We can skip the formalities here," she said as I made to stand to attention and salute. I took the seat but sat upright professionally as she slipped back behind her desk. "Forgive my appearance, Dodgson. We are changing our uniforms for reasons that will become clear later. I do, however, have an urgent issue to discuss with you. As you are aware, our victory came at quite a cost in personnel. We've lost many officers. We've been making a short list of enlisted personnel we hope to commission to fill those roles. The Admiral was most insistent that we include your name on that list. Is that something you would entertain?" Addison asked.

"I'm honored to serve her in whatever way she sees fit," I said honestly.

"We want you to form a specialist unit willing to take on hazardous recon missions. We'll need you to go to areas we plan to attack and return with the information for our planning. I won't lie. It's highly dangerous as you and a few personnel will be sent behind enemy lines. Are you up to that, Dodgson?"

"Of course, ma'am, I'm a Marine."

Addison smiled. "We'll make the post official in a few days. There's going to be a special announcement by the Admiral today. Make sure you watch it and understand it. If you have any problems with it, come and see me. If you disagree with its content, there won't be any repercussions, but it will affect whether you receive the commission."

I left her office most curious about what Admiral Plural was going to announce, but I also wanted to share this with Helen. The time had come to see what her deal was, so I waited outside her quarters one evening so she couldn't avoid me when she got off duty. She was surprised and uncomfortable when she saw me.

"Hey H...H...Helen. We need to talk." I said gently.

She sighed despondently. "Yeah. I suppose we do."

She opened the door, and I followed her in. She tossed her work bag on the couch with the other trash and headed into the kitchenette area. "Want a coffee?" she asked.

"Might as well while we still c...c...can. Mr. Phelkar says they're going to start rationing it now that we can't get supplies from Earth." I said as I sat down. She didn't respond to this as she made the drinks. When she handed me the mug, I took a deep breath and just came out with it. "I don't n...know if you have any ideas of where we are g...going or if this is g...going anywhere at all." My voice was nervous and uneasy as I blurted it out. "You and m...me, I mean."

She sighed, took the mug from my hand, then placed both on the table beside her. She took my hands in hers and said softly, "They're giving me a commission, Emma, and that means anything between us'll be fraternization."

I saw a tear well up in the corner of her eye.

She looked startled as I sat down and pulled her onto my lap, my arm around her, looking down into that pale, brightly freckled, beautiful face.

"They've given me a commission too. So it won't be fraternization," I whispered.

Her eyes widened.

"Seriously?" She looked excited for a moment but then her face fell. "I'm gonna to be a captain. I'll still be your superior."

I shrugged, not letting this moment be spoiled.

"There're w...ways around that." I shrugged. "Let's get m...m...married."

Helen laughed. "Be serious, Em."

"I am b...being serious, Helen," I insisted with a laugh. "L...look at it this way. If we don't, we can't s...see each other. If we do, there's f...f...fuck all they can do. And if it doesn't work out, we get d...divorced."

Helen pondered this, and she gently laid her forehead upon mine.

"Let's do it." She barely whispered.

"Seriously?" I lifted my head to look up at her.

"Yeah, hun!" She grinned childishly down at me. "Let's get married." Then she leaned into me, and we kissed long and hard, and she started to remove my clothing when the alert went off.

Her wide-screen T.V. came on as it does with any emergency broadcast. We both looked up and saw the bridge of the Constitution. "Stand by for an emergency message from the leader of the free Solar System."

"Wow, that's quite a title she's given herself!" Helen muttered as she slid off my lap and stood to watch. Seconds later, I was standing at her side.

Mr. Phelkar was standing in front of a lectern dressed in a smart new suit and tie, looking most handsome. "This is Michael Phelkar speaking to you from the bridge of the U.S.S. Constitution. I present to you the new leader of the allied resistance forces, Jennacia Plularian."

The doors opened, and Admiral Plural entered, looking resplendent in a black nondescript dress uniform with no national insignia. The crew stood up to attention. As she stopped in front of the podium, she raised her hand to indicate that they should sit and then looked ahead. She paused and looked around at her crew before looking back at the camera and speaking.

"I pray that I come to you today as a beacon of hope. I have assumed command of the loyal remnants of the allied forces. You should have already heard about the great victory over the Europeans in the Battle of Deep Space. We emerged from it stronger and more committed to the cause of freedom than ever before, for I say to you now, as clear as I can be." Her voice rose aggressively, and she slammed a leather-gloved fist on the podium. Anger and passion were vehement in her eyes. "We completely and utterly reject the surrender of the leaders of the Pacific Alliance. We won't roll over like a dog under the tyranny of the European Union. We won't hide. We won't run. We won't capitulate. We did not ask for this war!" Spittle flew from her mouth. "I did not ask to sacrifice the lives of our young. I don't love war." She paused, then shouted, "I love freedom, and I will fight, bleed, and die to see that restored!" Her voice lowered. "It is not going to be easy. You are bloodied and bruised, but we have shown the Europeans that we will be the masters of our destiny. I say to you all," she raised a clenched fist and shouted once more. "Rise up! Rise up and be counted as a hero! Rise up and turn on your oppressors! We will be out here, growing in number every day. Taking the fight to wherever a European cowers and hides. We are battered, but we are unbroken. We will strike at the very heart of European domination. We will destroy every ship. We will destroy every base. We will destroy every European we encounter until no more Europeans are left. We will take no prisoners. We will pursue the enemy with our hearts filled with vengeance for the loved ones we have left behind on Earth. I dedicate myself, and I ask you to do the same, to the total eradication of the European Union. I don't bring you victory today, but I do bring you the promise of victory tomorrow. It may take months. It may even take years. I promise you, with everything that I am. And to you Peon scum out there. I am coming for you. The day will arrive when the European Union is no more than a footnote in the history books. This is total war, and we are coming home!"

"So, she actually did it! She's taken over." Helen said softly before looking up at me. "Emma, what is wrong?"

Tears were streaming down my face, although I made no sound. I just looked down at her.

"I'm so proud to be p...p...part of this, Helen. Aren't you just so p...proud of her? The Admiral, I mean."

She didn't respond at first, and her face was quite passive, but then she smiled. "I've worked with Jenna for several years, and when you've seen her in the ways that I have...Well, you see the reality beyond the legend. I have seen her at her highest and her lowest." She sighed. "I wish I could see her with your eyes, but I can't. I can't step back and see her as this woman who is the great Commander in Chief."

"Yet she is." I smiled, and I looked back up at the screen and watched as the new Admiral Plural shook hands with the senior officers. The love of Jenna Plural radiated in my heart. "We finally have a chance of winning this war, Helen, and she's going to lead us to it."

I didn't look back as I heard Helen sigh again. "I hope so, Emma, I really do."

******

We had to get our marriage approved, and I was nervous it wouldn't be, but it came back signed by Addison. And so, we did it. No pomp and ceremony. We just went and signed the papers and came out as civil partners. We moved into new married officer quarters, and it was a luxury compared to what we had been used to.

I was made to attend officer training classes supervised under the office of Commodore Addison. Mr. Phelkar was sorry to see me go from his staff, but even his work had been winding down as more and more of his duties got turned over to Addison. The classes were rather dull and more about protocol than leadership, although they tried to convince me the two were intertwined.

I was assigned new offices. Addison told me that I had the pick of any personnel for this new unit with a few exceptions. Such as, I couldn't pick Helen Tracker as my tech as she was now the head of fleet technology... well, that and she was now my wife, but you get the point.

The major positions to fill in the unit were Sergeant, Vehicle Specialist, Tech Specialist, and Weapons Specialist. Finding the Tech Specialist was the easy part. I simply asked Helen to pick someone from her team and assign her to me. It all went smoothly until I put in my request for my demolition expert. Katherine Andreas was an army veteran of about seven years. She was legendary among ordnance personnel for her ability to control explosives like it was an art form.

However, when I filed the paperwork and sent it to her current commanding officer on board the U.S.S. Defiance, I received a very curt response. Andreas was an essential part of his team, and he couldn't possibly spare her and thanked me for my interest.

I wasn't too sure how to react to this. As an enlisted grunt, I was used to being told no, but I've never been in a position before where I was told I could do something, and then someone else would refuse to let me do it. So I took the issue to Addison, but she was far from sympathetic.

"Of course, he doesn't want to give up his best personnel," she told me curtly. "No-one would; however, you have been given the authority to recruit her to your team, and you need to use that authority. You can't come to me whenever you face a hurdle. Now go get your demolitions officer."

Easier said than done. I wasn't ready for a confrontation with a senior officer, no matter how much authority I'd been given. It had been bludgeoned into me from the day I joined the Marines that I take orders, not give them, and it was hard getting past that.

So, steeling myself, I sent him a reply stating that the transfer of Katherine Andreas was not a request and that I expected it to happen in the next few days. I then moved on to recruiting my other personnel, which was not so problematic.

A couple of days later, Andreas's commanding officer hadn't replied, so it was my move again. So I looked up to see where he was stationed, and I arranged a fleet shuttle to transport me there. Upon arrival, he refused to see me stating he was too busy. This information was relayed to me through his assistant. To be honest, I felt somewhat flummoxed. It was quite a quandary. The man outranked me. Yes, my authority came directly from Addison, but...I decided to bluff. Looking the P.A. straight in the eye, I said, "Very well, although I'm sure Admiral Plural will be most disappointed in his failure to assist me."

I then headed out to the shuttle dock but was barely down the corridor when the P.A. caught up with me. "It would appear that the captain has found a space in his itinerary and can see you now."

I grinned, then composed myself with a grim face before I turned back to him. I followed him back into the reception, and he led me to a back office.

The first words out of the mouth of the elderly Captain Tanner were, "You can't have her. She's a vital part of my team and doesn't want to leave anyway."

I raised an eyebrow, and after a dramatic pause, I replied, "On the latter p...part of that, isn't it irrelevant? While the choices of personnel can be c...considered, they're not the deciding f...factor in any posting. On the former, I have b...b...been given liberty to ch...choose any personnel for my team that I wish."

He glared at me, his face reddening with anger. "You're barely out of diapers, Lieutenant. I've run this unit for twenty years, and we're an elite tactical team."

I raised a questioning eyebrow. "I may be b...barely out of d...diapers, Captain, but I *am* out of them."

"You can't even string a coherent sentence together, girl," he angrily waved a dismissive hand toward me. "How do you expect to command and perform in a firefight?"

"Th...that is n...not your c...concern, Sir," I responded.

He then seemed to have a realization and sat up, wagging an accusatory finger at me. "Your one of those Theta squad promotions, aren't you? That damn GenMod putting her cronies into powerful positions."

Anger now welled up within me. "That is neither here nor there, Captain." My eyes narrowed. "I would choose your words more carefully, Captain. You sound like an insurrectionist, and *that* is not something tolerated."

"When you manage to dry your ears, Lieutenant, you learn that obedience to the chain of command does not mean you have to agree with that chain of command."

"You're right. However, you are obligated to maintain respect, Captain. Jenna Plural is our leader, whether you like it or not, and I am commissioned to put together a team of which Katherine Andreas will be part. If you wish me to take this higher, I will, but trust me, neither Admiral Plural nor Commodore Addison will appreciate being dragged into what should be a simple crew redistribution issue. Am I making myself clear, Sir?"

He glared at me and looked as though he was going to protest further but gave up. "I will complete the paperwork tomorrow and send Katherine to you."

"I would appreciate it if you would do it t...today, as time is of the essence." It wasn't. We had no mission prep scheduled, and several of my team had to complete duties before moving over to the Constitution, but I wanted to push this little shithead.

"Very well, Lieutenant." He sat back in his chair and heaved a weary sigh. "I'm getting too old for all this bullshit. I should have retired several years ago."

"That might have been a good idea, Sir, as it is no longer an option."

"What is that supposed to mean?" He narrowed his eyes at me.

"Well, Sir, the fleet is no longer getting supplied from Earth, and resources will be stretched thin. There'll be no room for passengers, is all I'm saying." Before he could respond, I concluded the conversation. "I expect to see Andreas before the end of the week. If I don't, I'll list her as AWOL and order her immediate arrest. Do we have an understanding?"

I waited for the reply, but he simply said, "You're dismissed, Lieutenant."

I smiled, thanked him, and returned to the U.S.S. Constitution. I was fuming at the disrespect he had shown both me and our leader. I wanted to do to him what I excelled in doing, but I had a better idea when I returned to my office. I put in a report to Charlotte Kensett. Two days later, I heard he had been relieved of command, and I never heard of him again.

Chapter Sixteen

The Icy Wastes of Hell

M y Sergeant came as the result of a recommendation by Captain Addison. Audra Pentauk had recently been serving under the also recently promoted Stacey Grant, but this was hardly a glowing reference for me. However, I considered it inappropriate to not accept my commanding officer's suggestion. I picked out the rest of my team, and I received no further direct objections, but I did hear that complaints were being sent up the line to Addison, who, as I understand, didn't respond to them in a very friendly manner.

With everything complete, I sent my list up to Addison for the formality of her stamp of approval. It was done and dusted. I was commander of a new elite force of commandos. Now, I had to turn them into a team.

Winning over the hearts and minds of your troops is probably the hardest task for an officer in any military branch. It's not enough that you get their obedience. You have to get their trust, which doesn't mean becoming their friend. However, an officer's most powerful tool is their Sergeant. If the Sergeant can work well with you and your people, you're halfway there. Pentauk turned out to be an excellent Sergeant with the right mix of authority and approachableness for this.

When I first met the team, they looked like a little ragtag bunch. I had taken them from all the services – Navy, Army, Air Force, and Marine Corps. I had scheduled a meeting in one of the many cargo holds on the Constitution to begin our first prep sessions. I still didn't have an officer's uniform, so I arrived in combat fatigues with my corporal stripes removed.

Another hill I had to climb was that I was an officer via a field commission. Many troops have a hard time seeing formally enlisted personnel as commanding officers.

As I entered, they were all sitting around the room chatting away. The team was fourteen in total, and I'm not going to name them all unless it becomes important as I progress. For the most part, just try to remember Pentauk and Andreas. The moment she saw me, Pentauk barked out for everyone to stand to attention. They did so in a strict military fashion except for one. A short girl in her late twenties with a shaggy mane of badly waved hair and thick eyeliner sluggishly got to her feet. I chose to ignore it for now and introduced myself.

"Ladies and g...gentlemen, I am Lieutenant D...Dodgson, your new c...commanding officer, as I'm sure you're already aware. This unit has been c...commissioned at the direct request of Admiral P...Plural. It is my intent not to let her down. We will become the ultimate f...fighting unit in this flotilla. We'll be the first on the g...ground and the last to leave. We will go where no one else would d...dare go. You are the best, but you're g....gonna be better."

The short girl raised her hand. I don't know if she thought she was in high school, but I decided to indulge her. "Yes, what is it?"

"Meaning no disrespect, ma'am," she said, meaning she was just about to disrespect me. "While I readily admit we are the best, I'm wondering how someone who's not a year out of boot camp will command us. Especially one who can't even give a coherent order."

Pentauk was about to put her down, but I raised my hand. "What's your n...name, Corporal?"

"Andreas." She replied.

Ah, of course, it was. "A fair question. We're in a t...transitional period. Many people need to get used to the new ch...chain of command and our new leader. Some even think we should c...capitulate to the enemy. I have proven my...my...myself to the Admiral, and she has chosen me more for my loyalty than m...my experience. I don't need to n...know how to do the things you know. I just need to know what n...needs to be done. I'm not asking you to t...trust me, but I ask you to g...give me the chance to earn your trust. As for my st...stammer, it will not be an issue."

"That sounds good," Andreas said but added. "If you're arranging a picnic, but we're putting our lives on the line here, we can't worry about trusting you on the battlefield." A few murmurings of agreement flittered around the room.

"I understand your c...concern. However, these are desperate t...times, and we cannot expect things to g...go along the way they used to. We have to adapt to survive. We have n...no home base. No one is going to refill our ammunition. No supplies are c...coming from Earth or any of the other colonies. At least not yet. We are in the greatest f...fight of our lives. We do, or we d...die. However, put your f...faith in me, and I will not p...prove faithless."

The girl nodded. "If you're so confident, would you be willing to do a deal with us?"

"I'm willing to listen to what you want to propose?" I said uneasily.

"We do one mission with you and after that, if we're uncomfortable with your command, you allow us to decide whether to stay with you or not." She locked eyes with me.

I pondered this. "It is r...rather unorthodox, and my superiors will n...not like it, but yes, I'm confident enough to do that d...deal with you."

Addison did not like it. She chewed me out for fifteen minutes before she even let me speak. "I don't know what Jenna will say about this."

"To be honest, m...Ma'am, I didn't plan on t...telling her," I smiled, but Addison didn't reciprocate. "They raised some good p...points about my experience, and to be honest, I think I need to prove m...myself to them, to you, and to the Admiral."

Addison sighed. "Maybe you're right. I don't think so, but I'm going to trust you on this."

"Think of it this way, C...Commodore. If our f...first mission succeeds, they'll want to st...stay with me. If it fails, we'll all be d...dead."

Addison grinned. "Fair point."

A couple of days later, I was summoned to a conference meeting with Admiral Plural. Present with her were Addison, Kensett, and Helen. A technician called Ryan Baxter was also present at the request of Helen.

I felt somewhat excited because it was clear that this would be a mission briefing. My first true test of command.

"As you know, one of our biggest problems is that we don't have a base," Admiral Plural began. "While we have some ships that can be converted into farming galleries, it won't be sufficient to support us. In addition, the manufacturing of ammunition and weaponry is also a consideration. Even if we were victorious in every battle, losing one or two ships every time will ultimately whittle us down to nothing." She activated the large screen on the wall. It was filled with the picture of an icy world. "This is Enceladus. A moon of Saturn lying within its rings. It is also an American base with diverse manufacturing operations designed to supply the outer world colonies. However, since the surrender, it has gone radio silent. It does not respond to our calls. We don't know if European forces have occupied it or simply that the Americans have hunkered down to wait this out or even if they are now actively accepting European commands as part of the surrender. It is a highly secure facility with about six thousand people. So it's more than just a production site or military installation. It is a living, breathing community." She looked back at me. "Your mission, Lieutenant Dodgson, is to take your team in there and find out what's happening. However, I'm leaving the mission open-ended, and how we proceed will be based on your report. You may find they remain loyal. There may be a European presence, or they may simply remain independent. Either way, I intend to take Enceladus and make it part of the new Confederation. We need that base and its production facilities and the ability to land the ships capable of landing to maintain fueling stations, etcetera."

She returned to her seat as Addison got up to continue the briefing. "The base is heavily armed. It has anti-aircraft weaponry, so we can't drop you at the base and will be compelled to drop you several miles away. This area of space is also heavily patrolled by European forces, mostly French and some German. As a result, we'll be using the captured Peon shuttle piloted by Captain Grant, accompanied by Mr. Phelkar, for his fluency in French. They will drop you off without landing, only returning if the mission is aborted. Of course, we hope to land and meet you there, if successful. You'll have to track across the icy wastes facing obstacles such as chasms and freezing temperatures below anything you could possibly encounter on Earth. It's not going to be an easy trip."

She returned to her seat, and Helen got up. "When you reach the base getting in isn't going to be easy either. The base is not designed for people to walk in and out. Most exits are for people to maintain repairs outside and conduct surveys and other experiments. It is pretty sealed off. Most doors should be heavily guarded. What is not heavily guarded but still sealed off are the exhaust tubes. They pump out any noxious gases or chemicals produced in the base, and we believe we can get you in there through the access tunnels used for maintenance. Of course, the doors will be locked, so I asked Ryan to be here. He is one of my best techs, or rather he is now one of *your* best techs." Ryan smiled at me, and I smiled back. "It will be his job to bypass the security of the doors and get you in. I'll provide him with equipment to assist with this task." She sat back down, and Jenna rose once more.

"As I said, I don't know what you'll find there. If possible, contact the American leadership and find out where their loyalties lie. If possible, have them contact me, and I'll have Mr. Phelkar begin negotiations with them for some sort of agreement, or they may even outright join us. If not, you are to appraise the situation and gain as much information for us to take the base by force with a minimal amount of damage and loss of life. I'm going to give you a free hand here, Dodgson. You do what you think is necessary to find the easiest way to take Enceladus. If we don't hear from you within four days, it will be assumed you are dead, and we will reassess the situation. However, while you are there, there is a secondary objective."

She yielded the floor for Charlotte Kensett. "The base has another purpose. It is an outpost of the United States Department of Defense Research Division. Albeit through a private sector contract with Grant Industries." An image of an elderly man came up on the screen. "This is Doctor Benton McKay, a senior researcher in M.E.T. technology. Prior to the capitulation, my sources informed me that he had made some major breakthroughs. I don't know what, but we believe they could be very useful for the war effort. If possible, you ought to locate and extract this man."

"What if he doesn't co...cooperate?" I asked.

"You extract him with or without his cooperation," said the Admiral casually. "However, this is a secondary objective, and I'll leave it to you to decide if it can be done without jeopardizing the primary mission." She looked around the table. "I believe we've covered everything." There were general nods of agreement. "Very well. Do you require any clarification on anything, Lieutenant Dodgson?" I advised her that there was not. "In that case, this meeting is closed. Dodgson, stay awhile." As the room cleared, I found myself sitting alone opposite the greatest woman who ever lived. She waited patiently until the door closed and then looked at me. "How are you holding up, Dodgson?"

"I'm doing very well, Ma'am."

"I have to tell you, I've received a lot of flak from my advisors for giving you a commission and placing you in such a position of authority. I stand by my decision. I made it clear that I have complete and utter faith in you. This mission will not just reflect on you, but also on me. Fuck this up, and I'll look like an idiot." Her steely gaze locked on me. "And Dodgson, I *really* don't want to look like an idiot. Are we clear?"

"I won't let you down, Ma'am. You have my word on that." I said with all genuine sincerity.

Her affectionate smile returned. "I'm confident that you won't. I just wanted to reiterate how important this mission is. Good luck, Dodgson. You are dismissed."

Rumors that Stacey Grant had got Phelkar into trouble in the ship's ventilation shaft started to travel around. It made the captain even less endearing than I found her before. Men are weak individuals when it comes to seduction. Even someone as honorable as Mr. Phelkar could fall afoul of that serpent. Using her feminine wiles to seduce such a man and bring him down to her level disgusted me. However, it was made worse by the fact that she was doing it to the man our leader had claimed as her own. Surely, for as long as Jenna Plural was interested in him, he should have been off-limits to everyone. She was worse than a no-good whore.

With great reluctance, I was compelled to work with her on this mission. Fortunately, I didn't have to engage in conversation with her, and we piled into the back of the shuttle. She and Mr. Phelkar sat in the cockpit. My team strapped themselves into their seats.

I sat there looking through the door at Mr. Phelkar and the Jezebel. We were supposed to slip out amongst the traffic with our trip being an unregistered and unreported departure to ensure prying eyes didn't know what we were doing. As we waited, I saw her looking at him, and I felt a pang of anger. Grant needed to be eliminated for the good of all, and I pondered when I would get my chance.

We waited for over an hour until Grant found the opportunity to slip in behind another craft. We drifted out of the dock on dark energy repulsors. She then set a course for Enceladus, and we were on our way.

As Stacey Grant brought us down over the drop zone, she called back, telling us to get ready. She would have to drop us several miles from our target to avoid detection. We geared ourselves up in tactical E.M.U. suits checking each other seals. Then Grant sealed the cockpit door, and we all stood waiting for her call. When it came, I nodded to Pentauk, who nodded back and opened the outer door. As the vacuum enveloped us, everything went silent. My team's breathing over the comm lines was the only thing that could be heard. Standing by the opening, I looked down at the sheer white mass of ground before us. Our first order of business was to push out the equipment we needed. I then pulled the lever that released the bottom of the secondary cargo bay beneath us and dropped the all-terrain vehicle, in which we hoped would get as close as possible to the American base.

I slapped my first team member on the back, and he jumped out. Each followed in quick succession until, finally, Pentauk went too. I was alone and looked back at the door where Phelkar and Jezebel now hid behind. I sighed softly and then followed my team out of the doorway.

The gravity of Enceladus was so low that there was no need for any form of descent apparatus. A parachute wouldn't work because there was no air, but there was neither the need for D.E. compensators. The descent was slow enough that we could land on our feet without assistance and completely unharmed. As I went down, I watched for all the different places I could see my team coming down. The ground was coming closer at a very slow rate. To give Grant her due, she had found the perfect place for our landing, a flat icy plane that stretched onto the horizon. Eventually, I landed on my toes and turned around to take in my surroundings. Although we were on a flat plain, the planetary body was so small that the horizon disappeared quickly. I could only see two or three of my people. I activated my commlink.

"Dodgson down and safe. By the numbers, all check-in."

Slowly but surely, each person checked in with me. Although the likelihood of casualties or injury at this stage was unlikely, I felt relief as everyone confirmed a safe landing. "Pentauk, bring everyone into the t...t...terrain vehicle."

"Yes, Ma'am," came her reply, and she quickly snapped orders to the other troops and transmitted the vehicle's locator beacon. I looked up into the sky. I could make out the dim light of Grant's shuttle as it disappeared back up into space. I then checked the vehicle's location myself and headed in that direction. The walk to the vehicle took about twenty minutes across the sheet of ice, and it was lucky the spikes in my boots could grip its surface; otherwise, it would have been like trying to cross over an ice rink. I met up with two of my men en route, and slowly but surely, we all came together at the large vehicle. It had landed on its side, but it didn't take any effort to push it over onto its treads. All but two of us climbed inside, and Pentauk took the driver seat, as I slipped into a chair amongst my men lined up against the wall. Pentauk turned on the engine and checked the navigation system, and slowly we started to move out.

CHAPTER SEVENTEEN

TECHS

The first order of business was to pick up our equipment, and we spent about an hour following the locator signals with the two troopers jumping off of the vehicle to grab the equipment and stack it on the roof.

"That's the last of them," Pentauk informed me.

The two men on the roof climbed inside. When the entry hatch was sealed, Pentauk released air into the vehicle, and once the computer beeped confirmation that it was safe to do so, we all started to remove our helmets.

"Let's head out toward the b...base, Sergeant," I commanded.

"Yes, Ma'am," she replied and a few moments later added, "Course laid in. We're on our way."

The vehicle was not very fast. It was designed to get over difficult terrain, not to rush us into battle. My troops engaged in idle chatter as we traveled, but I didn't engage. I was startled when I heard a constant pounding of some things hitting our roof very lightly. I rose from my seat and went to the front, slipping into the passenger seat beside Pentauk. "What the heck is that?"

"I think it's ice, Ma'am. Look!" She pointed ahead and to the left. Looking out, I could see the massive geysers erupting so powerfully that they disappeared up into space. What was hitting us was the ice, as it slowly fell.

"The beauty of G...God's creation is beyond description," I muttered.

I was unaware that I had said this out loud until Pentauk replied, "You can say that again, Ma'am. Wow!"

Indeed, I can't describe the beauty of that moment. I don't have the fancy words of Mr. Phelkar or even the colorful descriptiveness of Stacey Grant. You'll just have to trust me. This was amazing to behold. Disappearing into space, these geysers belched forth water from the planet's core. I continued to stare at it as we moved along, and my team took turns coming up and looking from the doorway of the vehicle cockpit. Their gasps of awe pretty much summed everything up. Then the land began to become hilly and then rocky. The vehicle began to struggle, and I decided it was time we should stop for the night.

Slipping back to my team and retaking my seat with them, Pentauk joined us. I had one of the privates break out the rations and serve them to everyone. Solid blocks of neutrophil gunk. Tasteless and barely digestible.

"Well, it's not the most c...comfortable place to sleep, but do your b...best. It's probably the last ch...chance we're going to get until this m...mission is over," I told them. They were all veterans and wouldn't exactly be unused to sleeping in strange places.

I didn't get much sleep, not because of discomfort but because my mind was on the mission ahead and not knowing what we would find. Part of me was eager to find the base intact with the welcoming arms of American civilians, but another part was eager to put my training to use and fight our way to the heart of the community.

As dawn approached, I made my way up to the passenger seat at the front of the vehicle. I say dawn, but I refer to the time on our watches, rather than the positioning of the moon we were on. I gasped as I could now see Saturn overhead. The most beautiful sight in the solar system filled the sky. Pentauk soon joined me, and she was also taken in by the sight, with a broad smile on her face. I smiled at her. "Let's get m...moving, Sergeant."

"Yes, Ma'am."

Had this been on Earth, there was no way that the vehicle would have made it up over the mountainous terrain we now traversed, but with the low gravity, Pentauk was able to bounce it over the more tricky or steep areas. When we finally reached the top, we stopped and looked down across the wastes to see the vast dome structure of the American base. It was hard to get a perspective of how far away it was with the curvature of a moon this size and the lack of any other topography. I had to look down at the navigation screen to be told how many miles away it was. However, what caused me to sigh was the sight of a chasm between us and the base. It wasn't particularly big, but big enough that there was no way the terrain vehicle could jump it, even if I wanted to try, which I didn't.

Pentauk moaned.

"It was too good to be true for this to remain a smooth ride, Ma'am," she muttered.

"Agreed." I chuckled. "Come on, get us d...down there as close as you can, and I'll let the team know what's happening once we're there."

"Yes, Ma'am."

The mountainous outcropping's descent down the other side proved harder than the actual climb. It was only the consummate skill of Audra Pentauk that stopped us from bouncing off of it. Slowly but surely, we reached the glacial plane again. It took about another hour to reach the chasm, but I didn't need to inform the team, for all the bouncing around had ensured everyone was awake.

Pentauk scanned the topography to ensure that the closer we got to the edge of the chasm, the ice remained solid for us. She ultimately got us just a few feet away from the edge.

"Okay, this is as f...far as we go with the vehicle. We're g...going to have to abandon it here. Hopefully, we can p...pick it up again once our m...mission is over." By the look on the faces of my team, they didn't give a shit about leaving the vehicle behind. I was thinking about the fleet's limited resources and that abandoning such useful equipment on a single mission was a waste.

We resealed our helmets, and the air sucked back into the system, and once more, the hatch was opened. Pentauk went first, followed by my team, and finally myself.

It looked weird and silly to see my team putting equipment packs on their backs that were four or five times the size and weight of what they could carry on Earth. I jumped off the roof with no more difficulty than if I was stepping off a sidewalk curb. I walked up to the edge of the chasm and looked down, my stomach queasy at seeing the long drop into darkness. Then looking across to the other side, about twenty feet away. I turned and waved one of my people forward to join me. "Do you think you c...could get a harpoon into that side?" I asked.

He looked at me quizzically. "Sure, ma'am, but with this gravity, we could just jump it."

I hope he couldn't see me blush at my stupidity when he said this. I surely wouldn't forget him humiliating me this way. "Show me," I said coldly and stretched out my hand to indicate across the chasm.

He nodded, and, taking a run, he jumped into the air, sailing up a considerable distance before he started his descent, clearing the chasm by at least a further twenty feet. With that, I waved off the rest of my team and one by one, they leapt over to the other side, with me bringing up the rear. As I floated across, it felt strange as I arced and went down again, landing nimbly upon my toes. Then we made the steady march toward the base. As we got close, I tried to communicate with it again by radio, but all I got back was static. Slowly the dome grew in size, and eventually, we stood at its outer wall.

I studied it briefly before turning to Katherine Andreas and saying, "How about the possibility of b...blowing a hole in this wall for us to g...get inside?"

She looked at me incredulously. "Even if I could, which I can't, you would cause decompression and kill anyone on the other side," she said, causing others in the group to chuckle, much to my further humiliation. "However, these domes are designed to resist an aerial bombardment, so I wouldn't even scratch it with the ordnance I have."

"It was j...just an idea," I muttered.

"Yes, Ma'am," she replied in a most condescending tone. I caught the gaze of Pentauk, who was looking at me in wide-eyed disbelief. Damn it to hell. I would have to step it up if I had any chance of winning this team over.

I started walking along the outside of the wall. I got quite a distance before looking back, and saw my team was still standing where I'd left them. "Come on," I commanded. They looked at each other before very begrudgingly following on. We continued for about an hour until we came to one of the exhaust ports we had been told about. Its vast jet was chugging away silently, and a faint green plume was expelled. This would be a fan on Earth, but with no air, such a device was useless here. Instead, everything was suctioned out.

"I was hoping this wasn't g...going to be active," I said to Pentauk on a private line.

"Well, at least it means this base is operational. There *are* people inside," she replied. With no air being expelled, walking up to the fan in a vacuum proved very easy, and I spotted the small maintenance hatch leading through to an airlock at its side.

I turned to Andreas. "Is there a problem with b...blowing this?" I asked sarcastically.

"You could try just opening it first. That's why we bought a tech, isn't it?" she said irritably.

It was my turn to be vitriolic as I replied. "There is n...no way to open it on this side." I indicated the lack of any lock or handle.

Andreas slouched over. "Okay, everybody. Stand back," she said. "You won't see or hear it, but y'all damn well feel it if you get in its way."

We all backed out, went around the corner, and waited impatiently while she set up her explosives. Minutes later, she came and joined us and stood with arms folded, glaring at me for a reason I couldn't comprehend. Sixty seconds later, pieces of debris flew out silently into our view.

I slipped my officer's pistol from my holster and nodded for the others to ready their rifles. "Okay, t...team, we have access to Enceladus Base. We enter with caution. And be ready for anything. And for f...fucks sake, don't shoot any civilians, regardless of nationality."

"How in hell are we gonna know the nationality of civilians?" Andreas said to the laughter of the rest of the team. I was *really* starting to hate this girl.

I just replied. "M...move out."

We headed back into the vent, stepped over the debris caused by the explosions, and entered Enceladus Base.

The darkened corridor ended at the opening of the airlock. I stood aside as the technician, Baxter, stepped up to the door. It only took a few minutes. The tech stepped back, the door swung open, and we entered the airlock. The door closed behind us, and the compartment started repressurizing and filling with air automatically. I reached out to unfasten my helmet, but Pentauk suddenly grabbed my arm. "Ma'am, we have no idea what the conditions are on the other side of that door. We could decompress again." My team began muttering and chattering until Pentauk snapped, "Shut it, troopers." Silence fell once more, and I realized I was losing any hope of respect from this group and would need to do something soon to restore my authority. The technician worked on the inner airlock, and there was that slight hiss as the door came open and the different air met each other. This led us to a maintenance shaft.

The shaft was large enough for us to walk upright. And we continued along it for about ten minutes. We found the door at the end, but it was sealed from the other side. I hesitated, ensuring I checked all our options before returning to Andreas. She nodded, and we all stepped back out of the way as she came forward. She stared at the door momentarily, then looked back at me and shook her head.

"This door is at least six inches thick. It's designed to withstand decompression explosives. If I blow this, that won't leave much of this shaft behind, and we'll kill ourselves."

I sighed and bit my lip, pondering what to do next. Some'll say it was a coincidence, but, like it was divine intervention, the door began to open.

"Deus ex m...machina," I muttered.

"Huh?" Pentauk responded as we brought up our weapons.

"N...never mind."

There stood a surprised-looking tech in overalls and an ungainly tool kit about her belt. She couldn't have been older than me, and she slowly raised her hands with wide eyes at the sight of us.

"Oh dear!" she muttered softly. American accent, Tennessee...good.

"Name, rank, and number." Pentauk barked at her.

"Amy Bessinger." She replied in a voice that could only be described as fear as Pentauk slowly and gently guided her back so we could step through the entrance. "I'm a civilian and don't have a rank or number." She hesitated. "Well, unless you want my social or Grant Industries employee number. But I'm a First Technician if that helps."

I looked down at her belt to check for a weapon. I nodded for Harris, one of my team, to search her. He stepped up to her and made her stand facing the wall, with her hands raised high upon it. He returned his rifle to his shoulder and went through her tool kit, then patted her down. He nodded to me that all was okay and stepped back. However, I didn't relax.

"Turn around slowly. We are with The United States M...Mar...." I started to say until Pentauk corrected me with a nudge. "I m...mean the Solar C...Confederation Special Operations Team. We're here to c...claim this base."

Amy looked at me with wide eyes and gave me a little shrug.

"Well, okay then," she said softly.

Again, I realized how stupid I was, announcing this to what was little more than a grease monkey. "Are you able t...to take me to someone in a p...position of authority?"

"Well, I can take you to my manager," she replied. "Though I'm not sure he can help you any more than I can."

"Please don't hurt her." I spun about with my weapon to see a young man approaching, his hands raised in a peace gesture. Tall, Hispanic with gentle features, and dressed similarly to Bessinger.

"Identify yourself." I demanded.

"Angel Mendez. Senior technician," he said abruptly. "I should warn you. You will not get a warm welcome here. The hierarchy of this base has taken advantage of the surrender to become fully independent."

"But this is a research and industrial base. It's not even a colony," Pentauk said, stepping up beside me.

"Well, it's a little more than that," Mendez said uneasily.

"Explain," I said curtly.

"May I ask that you lower those weapons? I can't speak for Amy here, but I consider myself a loyal American. I want to help if I can, but I am not sure what I can do."

"Hey, if you can get me out of here, you can count me in, too," Amy said eagerly.

"Well, there are two d...d...different definitions of a loyal American these days," I said cautiously.

"I'm not sure what you mean." Mendez frowned.

"Do you support or oppose the surrender of the United States and the P...Pacific Alliance?" I asked.

"Ah, now is that a question where you'll shoot me if I don't answer correctly?" He said uneasily.

"Possibly. But I would almost d...definitely shoot you if you don't answer." I smiled at him when I said this.

"Well, it's rather a game of Russian roulette then, isn't it? Here is my answer. I support whoever has the best interests of my people at heart. I am yet to be convinced either side has our best interests at the forefront of their minds."

"F...Fair enough." I gestured for my team to lower their weapons, and they complied. Mendez sighed with relief, and he and Bessinger then led us back to what looked like a small warehouse filled with work benches covered in broken equipment, which the techs were working on. Several stopped working and stood up to stare at us as we entered, and soon a small group was gathered around us.

"After the fall, the powers that be closed us off from all contact." Mendez was telling us. "Things here are not what you would expect."

"Shut up, Mendez. You're going to get us all killed." An older woman snapped at him.

"Do you want to stay on this rock for the rest of your life, Kendra?" Amy snapped back. Kendra hesitated and was about to say something, but backed down and lowered her head.

Mendez looked back at me. "This place is supposed to be run by an Australian company called Grant Industries which was contracted to the U.S. Department of Defence. However, after Australia fell to the Peons four years ago, we kinda became forgotten, and the cartel took over. For several years, this base has been used by a syndicate called the Brotherhood of New York."

"How is that even possible?" Pentauk asked disbelievingly. "To even land here, you had to have high-security clearance."

"Yes," Amy laughed. "And in an ideal solar system, there'd be no such thing as government corruption. We're not living in an ideal solar system."

"What is the n...nature of the legal activity here," I asked as I sat at an empty table and indicated for my team to relax.

"On the minor side, we are talking about smuggling goods for tax evasion," Kendra spoke. "Ships stop here and unload their cargo. Another ship picks them up and takes them to the next port of call."

"And on the major side?" Pentauk asked.

"Tech running. The primary research here is weaponry and a black market has been running out of here unchallenged for the longest time."

My eyes widened. Tech running was a serious crime. It was selling military tech to the private sector or even possibly the enemy. Anything from small arms to computer systems and missile weaponry. At best, it was theft and unlicensed arms dealing; at its worst, it became treason.

CHAPTER EIGHTEEN

THE SCIENTISTS

"Okay, what are we t...talking about here?"

"Schematics," Mendez said quietly as if we could be overheard. I shrugged and looked questioningly at him, not knowing what he was talking about other than the definition of the word schematics. "Research is conducted here on developing new and interesting ways to kill each other, and then the plans get sold in a black-market auction to the highest bidder."

"How could the U.S. government not notice it's not getting the tech that it's paid for?" Pentauk asked.

"Oh, it gets it eventually, maybe a year or two after the schematics have been sold. It's not exactly hard to delay research or at least show that research has been delayed."

"Are you telling me that there's tech here that could have helped us win this war being held back for someone's bank balance?" I asked, unable to hide my growing anger.

"Well, that's how it worked over the last few years, so yes, I guess there's probably tech here that's been held back. Obviously, someone of my level doesn't know the specifics," Mendez told me.

I glanced at Pentauk, who looked seriously shocked, but I remembered something and looked back at Bessinger and Mendez. "My secondary m...mission is to find a scientist called McKay. He's s...supposedly r...researching advanced M.E.T. technology. Do you know him?"

He glanced uneasily at Bessinger, who looked down at her feet guiltily. "Not much more than a good morning basis, but yes, I know him," he replied.

"I need to see him."

"Well, good luck with that. But as soon as the powers that be find out you're here, they'll be out to kill you," Amy said. "They see the war's end as a profit loss and believe that by going independent, they can take advantage of the emerging nations out of the chaos."

"Exactly who are these powers that be?" Pentauk asked.

"The science quorum," Amy answered.

"Well, I hardly think a bunch of scientists will have much effect against us," Pentauk said, more hopeful than convinced.

"Yeah, I don't think you understand," Mendez said, almost sounding conspiratorial. "They aren't really scientists. It's a cartel front, and with the considerable stipend paid out under the counter to the security staff. When they stopped getting paid by Grant Industries, they gained their unwavering loyalty."

"I don't give a f...flying f...fuck if they are boy scouts. It's t...time to retire them and their activities."

"Can we assume you would be willing to help us in that endeavor?" Pentauk asked.

He hesitated and glanced at Amy. She nodded back at him.

"If it's going to get us off this rock, then I'm in." she said determinedly, and there were a few murmurs of approval around her.

Mendes sighed. "Well, it would appear that Enceladus Space Tech Division Two is at your service, ma'am."

About an hour later, we were out of our EMU suits, and the techs had fed us. It was nice to have something that wasn't basic military fare. We were relaxed and drinking coffee as we carried on talking.

"What is the military complement of this base?" Pentauk asked.

"Actually, none," Mendez informed us. "When Grant Industries took over, their corporate security replaced the military. When the surrender of the United States came over the line, most bugged out."

"Why d...didn't you go with them?" I asked.

Mendez looked at me as if that was a strange question, but he replied casually. "Enceladus Base may not be much, and it may not be the most hospitable place in the solar system, but it's our home. Most of us have been here ten years or more, and we've raised our families here. Why would we want to go somewhere else?"

I could think of a hundred different reasons to get out of this shithole, but I replied, "I understand. However, I t...take it that you didn't expect your current s...circumstances to happen?"

"No, our main concern was this base being taken by the Peons. With most of the security gone, there is no one to man the defenses." And that, I realized, was why no-one fired upon us coming in, but I said nothing and let Mendez continue. "There was a lot of talk about officially declaring independence, but then the cartel started losing control, now that their security was limited. Most of the science divisions have barricaded themselves in the outer ring of the base."

"Why didn't you go with them since they are not the criminal element?" Pentauk asked.

Mendez snorted with derision. "Because the cartel basically told us we couldn't and made the consequences of us trying to very clear."

"We should tell them, Angel," Amy said. He sighed and nodded. "We've been running an underground railroad to get scientists out of cartel hands, to where they can be blocked off in the outer ring," advised Amy. "As it happens, there *is* one called McKay. The one you asked about."

I sat up, interested. "Where c...can I find him?"

Amy was about to answer, but Mendez suspiciously said, "Why do you want him? "

I had no obligation to answer this question, but I doubted he would continue helping us if I didn't. "He's working on some tech my superior is interested in obtaining."

Mendez sighed. "So that's the real reason you're here?"

"No, Sir," Pentauk put in quickly. "It is an objective of ours, but it is a secondary objective."

"Be honest with me, and I'll be more helpful," Mendez responded. "What is your true objective?"

Pentauk looked at me. I sighed and answered him. "We intend to m...make Enceladus base a part of the Solar Confederation. A place where we can repair our ships, rotate p...personnel, and to call a center of operations for the new war effort. The fight take Earth back has begun."

"And what about us?" Amy asked uneasily.

I fixed my eyes upon her determinedly to ensure she took me seriously. "Your skills will b...be invaluable to us. There's a p...place for you in the Confederation and we'll value that."

Mendez shook his head. "We're tired of war. It's over, and we just want to live in peace."

"Do you think the Peons will just let you live in peace?" Pentauk asked intently.

"They would take over this b...base with their military and use the research d...done here against us," I said. "There will be no p...peace. It would just be about which side you're on."

Mendez didn't respond to this, only looking at Amy with a dejected sigh as Pentauk added, "The biggest difference will be that you're volunteers, if you work with us. The Peons won't give you that option."

"I guess it is too much to ask that you would just leave us in peace?" Mendez said bitterly.

I balked at this. "You want us to liberate you from your c...cartel using *our* lives and *our* resources and expect us j...just to leave?"

"Even if we did do that," Pentauk said. "How long do you think it will be before the European Union starts landing ships here and taking over? You have two choices.

Become puppets for the Peons or join the force fighting for your liberty in the hope that one day you will be free to live here in peace."

Amy gave Mendez a sideways look. "They have a point, Angel. We heard that speech broadcast by Jenna Plural. She's standing up for us in a way the U.S. government never has."

Mendez sighed again and raised his hands in resignation. "Fine. What would you have us do, Lieutenant?"

"We n...need to take out this quorum's h...hierarchy. It shouldn't b...be difficult if they don't have military support." I replied.

"What sort of armaments do they have?" Pentauk asked.

"Standard police issue weaponry, I would think," Mendez replied.

Pentauk looked at me. "Handguns, assault rifles, shotguns," she said, as if reading off a shopping list.

"Agreed. However, they d...don't have our t...training. Still, we should proceed with the greatest caution." I looked back at Mendez and Amy. "Is there any way we c...can get to the administration center without encountering opposition?"

Mendez shook his head. "Most of the travel around this base is in pods through the transit tubes, but they're pretty locked down by the cartel."

"Can you get them running for us?" Pentauk asked.

He pondered this as he looked at Amy before looking back at me. "There's only one person here with that expertise, and I'm not letting you take her."

Amy looked quite annoyed and turned on him aggressively. "You may be senior tech here, but I think you can't speak for me in these circumstances."

"I don't want you getting killed, Amy," Mendez told her, looking a little embarrassed by her reaction.

"Look, let's be honest," Amy responded. "I know you've had the hots for me for a long time, but you should have gotten the message by now that it's never going to happen. This is not a decision based on your personal interest in me."

Mendez colored slightly and responded with a stammer that made mine look quite mild. I couldn't understand him, but Amy was not about to let him speak. She turned back to me. "Lieutenant," her voice was firm and determined. "I can bypass the lockouts. But I can't get it not to register on the central administration's computer systems. If we do this, they'll know we're coming and that you got help from us."

"Do you know any alternative?" I asked.

"We can always go through the maintenance shafts, but that would take you hours, and it's highly unlikely we'll get through undetected since various cameras monitor what goes on in there at various points."

I looked to Pentauk for her opinion. She looked back at Amy. "How long would it take a pod to get to the central administration?" She asked Amy.

"About fifteen minutes," Amy replied.

Pentauk looked back at me. "They'll know we're coming, but they won't have much time to mount a defense, and they won't necessarily know it's a military unit. Just that someone has activated one of these pods."

"However d...dangerous it sounds, it still seems like the safest option." I looked back to Mendez. "I would r...really like to see McKay, if it's at all possible?"

He nodded and rose to his feet. "Come with me."

He led Pentauk and me over to a large cargo container and opened the door. I looked at Pentauk, confused, and she just shrugged back at me. As we followed him into the dark, he lit a flashlight, and we could see an open hole at the back of the container, where it should have been up against the wall. It was hiding a room.

Three people jumped up nervously as we entered, two men and a woman. One of the men and the woman were not much older than me, but the other was far older, possibly in his seventies or eighties.

"What's going on, Mendez?" he asked nervously, eyeing our uniforms up and down.

"Relax, they're friends," Mendez replied.

"Is there such a thing now?" The young woman spat contemptuously.

"Only if you w...want them," I responded.

"And what if we don't want them?" she retorted with snarky suspicion.

"Relax, Tiffany." The older man said, with a surprisingly jovial tone. "Can't you see they're wearing the uniforms of the United States Marines? They're hardly going to be here to harm us."

"Nice to hear a v...voice of reason," I said, offering him my hand. "Lieutenant D...Dodgson. Pleased to meet you."

He took my hand and looked at me appraisingly. "Have you never tried to fix that speech impediment of yours?"

"It's not p...possible. It's been t...tried."

"Hmm! Impossible isn't a word that I enjoy. However, now is not the time to discuss it. Doctor McKay, at your service. These are my two assistants, Atticus Blake, and Tiffany Mahoney. Forgive Tiffany's attitude. She seems to have a corncob constantly stuck up her ass."

Mahoney viciously glared at him. Clearly, their relationship was not cordial.

"Are you here to get us out?" She asked, turning back to me.

"Eventually, b...but we're in great n...need of your assistance," I replied.

"Ah, Lieutenant Dodgson...and here I was starting to think we were getting along so well," he chuckled. "You're clearly after my technology, are you not? The new devices?"

"Well, that too. However, all we n...know is that you've m...made some advances, but we d...don't know what exactly."

He smiled proudly, turning around to lift what looked like a small suitcase from the floor, and placed it on a table. I moved over to stand next to him and looked down as he opened it. Small, flat, cylindrical objects about two inches thick and the width of an outstretched palm were carefully placed in the foam casing. He looked at us proudly, but I just stared at him and shrugged. He rolled his eyes.

"This is it. This is the new M.E.T."

I looked at Pentauk, who also shrugged, and we both stared back at him and then back at the devices. He muttered something about the dumb military with a sigh. "These are the prototypes of a revolutionary portable M .E.T. system. Each can carry up to three personnel for two and a half hours."

My eyes widened. "The m...military applications of that are potentially ph...phenomenal," I said.

"Not just military, but intelligence and many other applications to get people into anywhere you want them to go."

"But why only t...two and a half hours?" I frowned.

"It requires a lot of power, and unfortunately, that's the best I can get a battery to maintain a charge for. When the battery dies, it can no longer maintain the energy pattern. I was working on a way to release the inhabitants from the device automatically before that happened, but unfortunately, the surrender came, and I was unable to finish my work."

"Even so, this is an amazing accomplishment," Pentauk said.

He grinned at her with pride. But that grin dissipated when I said, "Admiral P...Plural will be exceedingly pleased with this."

He glanced at me, his face turning to cold rage. "You're with Jenna Plural?"

"Yes, Sir. We're part of the new Solar Confederation."

"Seriously?" He looked horrified. "Didn't you hear that woman's speech? She is a fanatic!" My face grew impassive as I glared at him. "She was talking about the genocide of entire nations!"

"She talks about freeing us from Peon tyranny," snapped Tiffany, throwing her hands into the air and turning away in frustration.

Atticus stepped between them. "Look, let's calm down. This isn't really the time to discuss politics."

"There is no way that I'm allowing my equipment to get into the hands of that...that...that *psychopath*!" McKay shouted.

"I don't think you have an option," I responded coldly, my anger brimming over.

He glared at me with crazed eyes.

"Oh, you think so?"

He spun around, snatching the case, and made to throw it hard against the ground. At the last second, he stiffened and dove to the floor, as I fired my swiftly drawn pistol at him. I grabbed the case with my other hand and placed it carefully back on the table, while Tiffany squealed and jumped aside. Atticus placed his hands on either side of his head in disbelief.

"What the hell are you doing!" Mendez cried out. "I bought you in here to save him. Not kill him!"

"I couldn't let him destroy that equipment," I said quite calmly. "It's too valuable to the war effort."

Tiffany recovered quickly, stating, "She had no choice. It's regrettable, but you were right. I heard Plural's speech too, and hell, I agree with her. Don't worry. I am sure I can finish his work."

"What are you going to do with us?" Atticus asked nervously.

"If you don't intend to stand in my way, I'll get you out of here and back to the fleet," I replied, my anger unabated.

"I wouldn't trust Atticus if I were you," Tiffany spat coldly. "He's a complete kiss-ass to the doctor."

"You bitch!" Atticus lunged at her, but I put my arm between them.

"Back off!"

"Hold up!" Mendez stepped forward. "I don't think the doc is dead."

I looked down and gave him a light kick. He groaned.

"Looks like you're r...right," I said casually.

"Let me go see if I can find a medic."

He started to head for the exit. "That won't be n... necessary, Mr. M...Mendez," I advised, as I looked down at the old man writhing in pain at my feet.

"Why not?" Mendez looked confused.

I aimed at the doctor's head, looked up at Mendez, smiled, and fired my weapon again. "He doesn't need a m...medic."

At my side, Pentauk muttered, "Oh, fuck!"

"Oh my God...she's a fucking psycho!" Tiffany cried out, jumping back. But as I shot her a venomous look, she raised her palms towards me in a gesture of peace. With a terrified smile, she said, "But the best possible kind."

That amused me enough that I decided to let it go.

I walked over to the table and picked up one of the new devices, feeling its weight in my hand. "How does it work?" I looked at Tiffany.

"Turn it on, place it on the floor, and get someone to stand over it," she replied.

I did exactly that, then looked at Atticus. "Get undressed."

But Tiffany smiled. "That's no longer necessary. The individual can be uploaded clothed and with their equipment."

"Nice!" I said, genuinely impressed. "Well, go on then. Stand over it."

With a sigh of resignation, Atticus stepped over it and disappeared without the typical M.E.T. flash of light.

I looked up at Tiffany. "Your turn."

She raised her hands in protest. "Look, I understand that you may not trust me, but I assure you, I'm on your side. There's no need to...."

I raised my own hand to stop her. "It's n...not about trust. I want to get you o...out of here alive. That'll be easier if you're not r...running around as a potential target."

She sighed but reluctantly stood over the device. After she disappeared, I looked down in amazement at the blinking light on the portable M.E.T. I crouched next to it and picked it up. It had a small clip on the back, and I fastened it to the back of my belt and turned to Pentauk, who was looking quite dazed about everything.

"Come on, let's m...move out. We have an appointment with whoever th...thinks they're in charge here."

CHAPTER NINETEEN

THE PEONS ARE COMING

As we returned to the warehouse, Pentauk reached out and grabbed me by the arm. "Ma'am, can I have a word with you before we get back to the others?

I looked back at her, genuinely curious about what her problem was.

"What's the p...problem, Sarge?

"What the hell was that back there?!" she snarled aggressively.

I still wasn't sure what she was referring to. I looked confused at the question, and her eyes widened as she realized I really didn't understand her objection. "You shot an elderly man who was incapacitated on the floor."

I couldn't help but laugh.

"My d...dear Sergeant, all I did was shoot someone who w...was clearly an enemy of the Solar Confederation and its leader."

"For fucks sake, Lieutenant Dodgson, he simply disagreed with her politics, and as far as I'm aware, that's still not a criminal offense."

"And j...just what would you have done, Sergeant p...Pentauk?" I responded with growing irritation.

She stood upright and at attention. "I'm a Marine, Ma'am. I act with honor. Semper Fi. What you did back there was dishonorable."

Before I knew what I was doing, I had my hands twisted in her collar, and I spun her around and slammed her down on one of the tables covered with technical junk, smashing her into a bunch of circuit boards. Almost crushing her beneath me, I pushed my face up against hers.

"Don't you dare question my honor, Sergeant! Who the fuck do you think you are?" I got up, pulling her with me, then slammed her back down again, barely noticing the techs and the troopers that were coming over to us. "Who the fuck is in command here?"

"You...are." She gasped out.

"Do we have a problem here, motherfucker?"

"No, Ma'am."

I let her go, and I turned to see the Marines and techs looking at me in shock.

"Nothing to see here. Gear up. We're moving out." I stepped away to collect my kit, not bothering to look back and see whatever reactions were.

The monorail was a single track of dark energy-powered pods that could hold up to six people. This bothered me somewhat, since I couldn't take the whole team in one go. This became an even bigger concern when Amy said, "I'm only going to be able to get one of these pods going. We're on reduced power."

I looked back at Pentauk.

"P...pick four of your best and send the rest b...back to Mendez," I responded irritably.

She nodded, and much to my annoyance, she chose Andreas amongst the four. Probably a good thing, since it was necessary to watch *that* one.

"Leave your p...packs. Arms only."

I turned back to the pod. At least it was surrounded by glass, and we could get a complete view of our surroundings.

Amy seemed to take forever to complete her work, but she finally stood up and gave me a nod and a smile. "You're good to go!"

I turned back to Pentauk, gave her a nod, and watched my people get into the back.

I looked back at Amy. "Thank you, ma'am. You're going to be a valuable asset to the C...Confederation."

She blushed lightly and nodded her gratitude without a word as I climbed into the front of the pod, next to Pentauk.

Amy slid the door closed and slapped the roof. "Good luck!"

She then turned back to the panel she'd been working on, and with the press of a few buttons, we slid along into the tunnel. It was slower than I expected, failing to temper the nerves running through my body. Amy was in control, and we slid straight through various stops on the way to the central core.

There was a small electronic map of the network overhead, and I watched as we got closer to our destination. If security were alerted, we would be sitting ducks.

215

As we came within one stop of our destination, I started my weapons check, and my team followed suit. It turned out that we were lucky. No one was waiting for us. I slipped my rifle over my shoulder and withdrew my officer's pistol as I climbed out first. We were in a small, clinically white reception area. There was a security desk, but no-one was seated at it. Clearly, our opponents were either not professional, or more undermanned than we realized.

Silently I pointed at two of my people and then at either side of the door. I nodded to the technician to move forward and check the door locks. He pulled some gizmo from his belt and attached it to the door. We waited while the small device buzzed, then he pulled it off and looked back at me with a nod before dashing back behind me.

I nodded to one of the regular Marines, and she stepped forward and hit the opening. The door slid open, and the gunfire began. I dived for cover as bullets rained over my head. Before I even got up, my team was returning fire. It'd seemed as if there were many opponents at first, but there were only two. They were dressed in civilian security uniforms and didn't stand a chance against battle-hardened United States Marines. They were dead within seconds.

I stepped into the corridor and stuck a bullet into each head with my snap pistol, just to make sure. I glanced back at my team.

"Any injuries?" That was a negative, and I moved forward into the long corridor to another door.

"Well, there it goes, our element of surprise," Pentauk said.

I didn't reply and nodded to the next door, and the process was repeated. This time, I stood further back behind the door. When no fire came, a Marine moved around the door, raised his rifle, and stepped in. "No sudden moves," he shouted. "Keep your hands in the air where I can see them." One by one, my people filed in, and I brought up the rear.

We were in a large operation center with dozens of people who looked like they were civilians. There was fear on their faces, which meant we had control. There were three rows of desks with computer screens, looking reminiscent of an astrodome flight control.

"Nice and easy, everyone and no one gets hurt," Pentauk instructed.

I holstered my pistol, stepped up to the center of the room, and stood with my hands behind my back.

"Who's in ch...charge here?" I asked, but no one answered. I sighed and repeated myself more curtly. "Who is in charge here?"

"We're American citizens!" An older woman snapped indignantly, giving me a defiant look, albeit with her hands raised high. "You have no right to do this!"

"In that case, you have nothing to worry about, now do you, ma'am?" I replied coldly. "However, you f...failed to respond to the lawful c...communications of Fleet Admiral Jenna P...Plural. That warrants an immediate investigation."

"Jenna Plural doesn't represent the American government!" A young man shouted at me. "She's just a nutjob

217

fascist renegade!" I heard the hatred in his speech. "Some weird fanatic."

I fixed my eyes on the young man who had just spoken to me.

"The Solar C...Confederation is now responsible for the welfare of all free p...people and American territories that are n...not in the hands of the European Union. That includes this b...base. Anyone who doesn't recognize that will be c...considered to be committing treason."

"But that makes no sense! The President is the governing authority." It was the old lady again.

"In surrendering, the President declared herself a traitor to the American people. We no longer recognize the authority of the Earth-based government, which now stands as a puppet of the Peons!" I said, trying desperately to temper my anger and not have everyone here executed on the spot.

"So, you expect us to follow that right-wing fanatic?" The young man snapped back.

I'd had enough of this, and to the horror of all around, including, I believe, a couple of my people, I pulled out my pistol and shot him. As his brain matter flew out the back of his head and he fell across his desk, panic started to rise within our prisoners.

"Stay where you are! Nobody move!" Pentauk shouted, and my troopers stood in front of the two other exits to ensure no-one made it to the door. I waited patiently for order to be restored. I then said quite coldly, "Does anyone else have a problem with the authority of Admiral Jenna Plural?"

No-one did. There was an old saying, I can't remember who said it, and it's quite crude, but it was very apt to our situation. 'When you've got them by the balls, their hearts, and minds will follow.'

I had them by the balls.

"I will only ask this one m...more time," I said in my most pleasant tone. "Who is in ch...charge here?"

Another long silence followed until someone plucked up the courage to speak. "You just shot him, ma'am."

I sighed softly.

"Well, who's n...next in line then? You're seriously t...trying my patience here."

"I am," replied the older woman, with a less cocky tone now.

"Name?"

"Catherine Marsters."

"Well, Catherine Marsters, you w...will sit down nicely with Sergeant P...Pentauk here and give her a full list of your p...personnel and security setup. You'll instruct all your security f...forces to disarm and find a decent p...place where my people can process them. If all goes well, f...further violence will not be needed."

At this point, I was startled to hear the door down the corridor we had entered open. As we spun around, we saw that it was another six members of our team. Good old Amy. This would make things easier.

I looked up at the corporal leading them. "Find somewhere we can hold the p...prisoners. Get a full list of n...names and occupations."

He nodded and headed out as I turned back to the civilians. "In a moment, C...Corporal Lincoln will be taking you out of here. Behave nicely for him, and n...nothing will happen to you. However, I want your Communication Specialist and your Environment and Life Specialist."

After a moment's hesitation, a young girl stepped forward. She looked barely old enough to vote. She raised her hand nervously. "I'm the Communication Specialist."

"N...Name?" I asked.

"Liz Nolan."

"Well, Miss N...Nolan, take a seat at your station, but d...don't touch anything." She nodded and complied. I looked around the room, waiting for the other person to own up. "It's b...been a long day, and I am very tired. I'm usually a very p...patient person. I will ask for the last time. Who is th...the Environment and Life Officer?"

A young woman elbowed the man at her side, and he reluctantly stepped forward. "I am, Miss. Brandon Meyer."

I nodded to him. "Take your p...place, Brandon, and again, d...don't touch anything."

The corporal returned and advised me that he'd found somewhere, and with a nod from me, he led everyone out except for the two that I'd held back.

"Okay, B...Brandon, I want you to give m...me a list of everyone in this base."

He looked at me, confused. "I can surely do that, ma'am, but there are thousands of people here." Behind me, I heard Andreas give a loud contemptuous snort at my expense. I felt the heat of embarrassment rising within me but replied, "If you'd let me finish, B...Brandon. I want a list of everyone *armed*."

"I can give you a list of people who are authorized to be armed, but I can't detect weaponry from here."

"Just do it, Brandon. You're starting to annoy me." I snapped.

"Yes, ma'am," he replied.

I stepped over to Liz. "Patch me into the C...Confederation fleet."

I gave her the frequencies and the codes required. Her hands darted over her keyboard until a voice echoed throughout the room.

"We are reading you, Dodgson." He knew who we were by the codes I had given him. "The Admiral was asked to put you straight through to her. Please hold the line."

There was a short pause before Admiral Plural's voice came across the line. "Good to hear from you, Dodgson. Report."

"Ma'am, we have c...control over the Enceladus Base," I replied.

"Understood." Her tone was intense and less pleased than I was expecting. What she said next gave me my answer as to why. "I'm sorry to tell you that you have the Peon fleet closing in on your location. I don't know if they know what you're doing, or if it's just bad timing. I've ordered the fleet to intercept them, but we won't be there before they reach you. What's the situation on the weapon systems?"

"Give me a moment to c...confer with our personnel here, and I will let you n...know," I replied.

"Go for it," she replied.

I looked over at Brandon. "Give me a sitrep of the weapon systems of this base."

"All weapon systems are offline to conserve power," he replied uneasily. I assume he was concerned about my reaction to this bad news.

"How long will it take you to b...bring them back onli ne.?"

He hesitated before replying. "I can't. At least not from here. They were manually disabled at the source."

I swore. "Did you hear that, Admiral Plural?" I asked her.

"I did." There was a pause before, very carefully, she said, "Dodgson. If you don't get those weapons online, the Peons will get a foothold on Enceladus, and we won't have a hope in hell of taking that base, or even picking you up."

"Don't worry, m...Ma'am. If there's a way to g...get them online, we'll do it."

"That's my girl. Let me know how you get on. Plural out."

A chill of excitement ran up my spine as she called me *her* girl. I was *not* going to let her down.

Enceladus Base had four primary guns that fired dumb-fire missiles. Naturally, this took quite a bit of power, but even so, it wouldn't have been the first thing I would have powered down, even if peace had been declared.

It shouldn't have been that problematic. A simple monorail ride to each emplacement, but things are never quite that easy, are they?

I had with me my tech and just two of my people. I wasn't expecting a problem. We would sweep in, reactivate the gun, and get out. The pod took us into the weapon control center. Of course, we couldn't just walk in there. I required the tech back at the Environment and Life Station to unseal the doors. It then took my guy less than four minutes to bring the massive cannon back online.

We repeated the process with the second, but everything went wrong while we were on our way to the third. We were zipping along with the monorail, when the faint hum of its D.E. engine suddenly cut out. I tensed and looked about as I gripped my snap pistol in its holster. We gradually began to slow down and eventually stopped. The onboard computer spoke to us in soft, reassuring tones that didn't in the least reassure me.

"Please stay calm. We are suffering a power outage. Maintenance drones have been dispatched, and we will be underway as soon as possible."

I pulled up my commlink. "P...Pentauk, what's going on?"

"Can't talk. We're under attack!" She came back, and I could hear the sound of rapid gunfire in the background.

"Fuck," I muttered. I turned to see if the door could open, but it was sealed shut to stop civilians from doing exactly what I was trying to do.

I turned to Baxter, the tech. "Can you do anything?"

"I can but try," he said cheerfully and climbed out of his seat and over the other two at the back, until he was at the rear of the pod. He pulled out some doohickey and ran it along on a panel. I got back on the radio. "P...Pentauk report."

"They've got us pinned down in the control center," she replied. "Station security decided to not comply with your instructions, Ma'am."

"How are you holding up?"

"We've lost three, but we've taken out more of them than they have of us!" She shouted.

"Do you think you can d...deal with that while we carry on with our m...mission, or do we need to return?" I asked calmly.

"You can carry on, Ma'am. Leave this to us."

As the line went dead, I looked back at Baxter. "How's it going b...back there?"

"Just another minute, Ma'am," he replied.

"Make it f...forty seconds." I snapped.

"Ma'am, if I say it will take me a minute, it'll take a minute," he told me.

"Hey, I was just saying what they say in the m...movies. Carry on." I shrugged.

He chuckled just as the door to the pod slid open. I jumped out, followed by my team, with Baxter bringing up the rear. I looked up and down the gleaming white tube, wondering whether it was best to go ahead or back. Having already visited two of the weapon sites, we were probably the furthest from Pentauk as we could get. "Let's move on. K...keep weapons ready and be p...prepared for anything."

We moved off down the tunnel, unaware of how long it would take us, as I didn't know the speed with which the pods travelled in the tube. After a few minutes, I radioed Pentauk again. "Sitrep?"

"They've thrown everything they have at us, but we're holding our own." Came the reply amid the gunfire.

"Casualties?"

"I have six down." As she said this, we came out by a monorail station. Not the one we wanted, but I decided then and there that it would probably be quicker if we cut through the base.

However, as we climbed onto the platform, I heard a bullet whizz past my head. There was a cry behind me, but I was already firing at the security officer who had come out of the doorway. Behind me, two other rifles opened up, bringing him down in a hail of bullets. As I turned back to my team, I looked down with frustration at the dead body of our tech. "T...Take off his equipment belt. We have to keep m...moving." I instructed one of the troopers. "Helen is going to be miffed. I lost her m...man," I muttered.

CHAPTER TWENTY

THE BATTLE FOR ENCELADUS

"Ma'am, this stuff is useless without someone who knows how to use it," one of the troops replied to me.

"We can worry about that once we g...get there. Come on, let's m...move out."

The three of us went through the doorway that the security guard had come through, very slowly and cautiously. It wasn't like I knew the way to the next gun. I knew it was on the outer ring, and if we kept to the outer edge of the base, we would come to it eventually. However, barely fifteen minutes later, our progress stopped at the end of the corridor, a sealed door. With no Baxter or Andreas, it looked like we would have to retrace our steps and find another route, until something occurred to me. I reached for the back of my belt and pulled off the small M.E.T. device. I studied it carefully until I was confident about which button was the recall switch. I clicked it and placed the disc on the ground, as it began a countdown from ten to zero. It didn't give me an option on who to get out of the device, but as I would later find out, it released people in reverse order. The last one in was the first one out, and I was pleased to see that it was Tiffany Mahoney that appeared in front of me.

"How long?" was the first thing she asked.

"Just a c...couple of hours," I replied. "We thought we had c...control of the base, but station security launched a c...counterattack on the control center. We have a Peon fleet headed our way, and I'm trying to get the guns back online, while my number one is trying to maintain control of operations. I've lost my technician, and I need your help."

Tiffany nodded. "What can I do?"

"For a start, you can get that d...door open."

At that, she simply smiled, turned around, and punched in some numbers on the keypad by the door, and it slid open. I muttered a curse to myself as I realized that, had I left her out of the M.E.T., she could have legitimately opened every door I required.

We continued on our way, keeping Tiffany behind me, but in front of the other two for her safety. We carried on for almost thirty minutes, alert for signs of danger. I was growing tired and frustrated. However, Pentauk finally called me with some good news.

"We've secured the control center, Lieutenant."

"Very g...good. Casualties?"

"I'm sorry to say that we lost seven, Ma'am."

"Understood. Maintain vigilance and c...carry on."

As the line went dead, I found we had arrived at the doorway of the third gun. Tiffany opened the door, and at my instruction, she brought it online. As we heard the massive gun grind into position, slipping out of the base's dome to point upwards, Pentauk came across the comms again. "Lieutenant, we'vve started picking up ships on our scanners' outer edge. E.T.A. about twenty minutes until they're in range of our guns."

"Understood. As soon as they're in range, you can start f...firing. Try to identify their command ships and m...make them the primary targets."

"In range" was a loose term when fighting in space, because there was no maximum distance you could fire at something. With no resistance, a missile could carry on forever. When we use the term in range, we simply referred to the least amount of time they'd have to respond. The further away a ship was, the more time it had to maneuver out of its way.

I was surprised we didn't run into anyone as we continued onwards. It was only afterwards that I found out that our opponents in the base had locked everyone down, having them remain in their quarters as they tried to deal with us.

Just as we were managing to power up the final gun, a base-wide communication sounded out. A thick Texan-accented voice boomed out, "This is Edward Granger, the official voice of the Science Quorum. I'm talking to the commander of the American forces currently acting against us. We do not recognize your authority here. This base has declared itself an independent state. We don't want to escalate the situation, but if you don't surrender now, we will activate the internal automated weapon systems and deactivate your Marine pin safety protocols. I give you five minutes to respond."

As the final gun moved into position, I looked around for an intercom. Finding one on the wall, I stepped up to it and hit the button.

"This b...base is now the official territory of the Solar Confederation, under Admiral Jenna P...Plural. Do you really think that they won't just send m...more if you take us out?"

The reply came with a haughty laugh. "Well, now that you've reactivated the external weaponry, any of your ships coming into range can be fired upon. However, it's not our wish to make an enemy of anyone. That's why we're giving you this chance to do the right thing and stand down."

"I d...don't know if you have access to l...long-range scanners," I responded. "But a P...Peon fleet is coming here to question your authority to remain in c...control of your base. You pretty much have two alternatives. One is to join us. The other is to accept your fate as a p...puppet state of the European imperium."

There was a long silent pause before he replied, "You appear to be right on that. We're willing to discuss terms with you."

"Have all your people stand d...down and not resist us. Where do you want to m...meet?" I demanded.

"I don't think it's necessary for us to meet in person. We can continue our conversation over the intercoms."

"So, you want us to leave you out there, so you can ch...change your mind once we've d...dealt with the Pe-ons?" I said snarkily.

229

"That's about the size of it," he replied. "What you're suggesting is I turn myself over to either you or the Peons for what could potentially be a long term of imprisonment or execution."

"That's n...not for me to judge. I'm not law enforcement, and your ultimate f...fate is not mine to decide unless, of course, you c...continue fighting us," I paused and then continued. "Honestly, all I care about is securing this base and m...making sure it doesn't fall into the hands of the enemy. It will be Admiral Plural who ultimately d...decides the fate of everyone in this station. I can assure you, sir, that she is very fair and equitable. And by cooperate, I mean, fully and completely."

"I see that I'm not going to have a lot of choice in this." There was another sigh and another pause. "Very well. I'll meet you in the control center with a small complement of personal security."

"N...No. Bring anyone armed, and w...we'll shoot you on sight. Am I understood?" I stated firmly.

"You're basically asking me to surrender myself to you?" He asked incredulously.

"All I am asking you is to s...cease being a threat to us, n...nothing more and nothing less. D...Do you agree or don't you? I've out of time to waste with b...banter."

Again, there was another irritating pause before he replied, "Very well, I'll see you in thirty minutes."

"One last thing before you go. Was it you who d...disabled the monorail?"

"It was."

"I would appreciate it if you reactivated it."

******

Back in the control center, it was a mess. Pentauk was arranging the removal of the bodies, and several consoles were smoking from fire damage. The Environment and Life Officer lay slumped over the console, his head to one side, his eyes staring at me lifelessly. I nodded to one of the Marines, and he pulled the man from the seat as I turned to Tiffany.

"Can you handle the environment and life systems?"

She shrugged. "I don't see why not."

She approached the console, looked down at the blood-splattered keyboard, and then back at me in disgust.

I just shrugged. "We all have to m...make do, ma'am."

She flopped into the seat with clear irritation, and with a last look at the keyboard and a disgusted sigh, she started tapping away.

I spun around as the door opened, and a small, portly, balding man stood in the doorway, raising his hands uneasily as he faced our raised weapons.

"Edward Granger. You're expecting me."

He was wearing an expensive business suit, and standing by his side was a tall young woman dressed in a feminine version of the same outfit with a knee-length skirt. She stood slightly behind him, and I correctly assessed that she was his personal assistant.

"C...Come in, Mr. G...Granger." I said curtly. "But keep your hands where we can see them until you've b...been searched."

He complied quite calmly, not showing any concern about his current situation. One of my Marines went over and frisked first him, and then the woman at his side.

"This is my personal assistant, Crystal Garrett." He introduced her, even though I didn't care. She was a thin-lipped, officious-looking woman who didn't appear to be as at ease as her boss. She looked around at each of my people with grim concern.

"I assume you're head of the criminal c...cartel operating here?" I asked Granger.

"That's quite an assumption, Lieutenant," Garrett said coldly.

"Fine, if you want to p...play games, then this conversation isn't going to g...go anywhere," I turned away, waving my hand dismissively at them. "You're clearly n...no science quorum."

"I'm only pointing out that Mr. Granger has never been accused of any crime in his entire life, and that doing so will incur serious repercussions." Garret challenged, fixing her steely gaze upon me.

"Really?" I couldn't help but grin as I turned back to them. "Repercussions with who exactly?"

The confidence in her face dissipated quickly. "Well. I...."

"Oh, I think we can dispense with the legalities of everything, Crystal. I think Lieutenant..." He looked down at the name on my chest. "Dodgson is *fully* aware of what and who we are. We're all outside any government rule at present."

"On the c...contrary, you are now considered s...subject to the authority of the Solar C...Confederation," I said curtly. "However, you should be aware that any c...constitutional rights you may have had as a United States citizen no longer apply. A state of m...martial law is in effect. And that, Sir, gives me a wide latitude to r...respond to...issues, as appropriate."

"That sounds like a threat, Lieutenant," the man replied uneasily.

"Oh, I'm j...just informing you of your rights," I replied, then added with a shrug. "Or rather, the lack of them." I then turned away and walked over to the communications officer. She looked nervous and was shaking a little, and she showed signs that she'd been crying. "Open up c...communications to the fleet."

She looked up at me. "Which one?"

"Ours, of course," I responded irritably.

She tapped a few buttons, and the communications officer on board the U.S.S. Constitution put me straight through to the Admiral. "Good to hear your voice again, Dodgson. How's it going down there?"

"I have to admit, I had a b...brief loss of control, and we lost six people." I knew better than to tell the truth of the matter. "A c...criminal cartel has been unofficially running this place. However, the leader has t...turned himself over to us."

"Well, that's not exactly how I would put it," stuttered Granger. "My understanding is I'm here under a flag of truce, not as a prisoner."

"Switch to visual communications." The Admiral instructed, and the communications officer complied without waiting for me to give the order.

The beautiful and graceful face of Jenna Plural appeared on the screen in large high-definition perfection. Judging from the background, she was clearly in her quarters and had her jacket off, indicating that she'd been off duty when I called. "I am Jenna Plural, fleet Admiral of the Solar Confederation. Who do I have the pleasure of addressing?"

"Edward Granger, chief executive of Enceladus Projects Incorporated."

"I thought so when I heard your voice. Well, Mr. Granger, I hope you're being cooperative with Lieutenant Dodgson, but I need to be assured. Be honest with me. I'll know if you're lying. Where do your loyalties lie?"

"My loyalties lie squarely with Enceladus Projects Incorporated. I'm not concerned about who's in government, but I'd rather not be subject to the European Union under the current circumstances."

Admiral Plural smiled. "Well, that's more honest than I expected." She sat back and folded her arms. "However, it would've been more honest if you'd admitted that you're a member of the New York Fraternity."

His eyes widened slightly, but he recovered. "How very astute of you."

She chuckled lightly at this. "Not really, Mr. Granger. Clearly you don't recall, but we've met before. That's why I had my colleague turn on the camera, so that I could be sure."

She called me '*colleague.*' My heart skipped a beat!

"I can assure you, that had I met you, I would've remembered such a beautiful woman as yourself," Granger said smarmily.

"Oh, it was over thirty years ago, so I doubt it," Jenna sat back in her chair and relaxed.

Granger grinned. "Ah, so the rumor is true. You *are* a GenMod, Miss Plural."

The Admiral's eyes narrowed. "I don't like that term, Mr. Granger. I'd rather not hear you use it again. And it's Admiral Plural, if you please, not 'Miss.'"

"Apologies, my dear lady. But I still don't recall you." Granger's smile didn't falter.

"You saved the life of my associate, Rockford Harlow."

The realization suddenly came to him. "Oh, *you're* Jenn? If I recollect, you were more than his associate. How is the old bastard? He must be knocking on eighty by now."

"He died in the Battle of Deep Space."

The was a hint of sorrow in her voice. I admit I was surprised. I'd met Harlow on The Chesty, but I would never have imagined he was that close to the Admiral.

"I'm sorry to hear that. He was a good guy," Granger said reflectively.

"That he was, but he regretted not being able to bring your gang down. However, the only reason I'm talking to you, and not having you arrested, is because of Rocky. Cooperate fully with Dodgson, and there may possibly be a role for your organization moving forward."

Granger looked quite surprised and raised a grey eyebrow. "You're willing to do business with us?"

"I assume you can negotiate on behalf of the entire cartel?"

"You assume correctly, Admiral Plural. I hold the rank of Senior Brother, and my word will be honored by all sectors of our community."

"Very well. Assuming we don't lose Enceladus to the Peons, I believe we can do business." With that, she turned her attention back to me. "How goes the situation with the base's defenses?"

"All weaponry is n...now online. We have four d...dumb fire cannons ready and waiting." I informed her.

"Excellent, that's good to hear!" The Admiral smiled. "We're on our way there as fast as possible, but you may have to hold out for a while before we can get to you." She was about to sign off when something occurred to her. "There's one other thing, Dodgson. We've lost contact with Captain Grant and Mr. Phelkar. Her last communication was that she was under attack. We have no idea where she is now. Do you know anything?"

"No, Ma'am. I saw her leave. She reported no signs of distress," I replied.

The Admiral sighed. "Okay, Dodgson, keep up the good work. Plural out."

Liz Nolan got my attention and hailed me over. "We're receiving communication from a European ship."

"What are they saying?" I asked impatiently.

"They're saying that they're landing with the authority of the United States government," she responded.

I couldn't help but grin at this. They weren't attacking. They were moving in with United States permission to

236

take control. They had expected to simply land and take over.

I turned to Tiffany. "Can you set the weapons to open f...fire when the first ships are in the moon's g...gravitational pull?"

"Not a problem," she smirked, with a tone of voice that meant, 'Yeah, give me something hard to do, would you?'

Then Pentauk approached me, looking concerned. "Isn't that cutting it a bit fine, Lieutenant?"

I turned, grinning like the Cheshire Cat from my favorite childhood story. "Don't you see? They think they'll get to c...come in as if we are happily c...capitulating to them. The c...closer we let them get, the more ships that will be in range."

Pentauk nodded, but still looked unsure.

"Trust me," I murmured gleefully.

CHAPTER TWENTY-ONE

A NEW AMERICA

I saw the Peons approach slowly on the scanners, keeping back, and I frowned, wondering what the problem was.

"You didn't respond to their hails," Tiffany said as if reading my mind. "Not hearing from you is making them nervous."

"But I don't speak F...French!" I snapped.

Tiffany rolled her eyes. "They sure make Marines dumb, don't they? This is an American base, and they *know* it's an American base. They don't expect you to speak damn French, stupid. They're expecting you to respond in English. You *can* speak English, can't you, Lieutenant?"

I flushed with embarrassment, as I turned back to the communications officer and told them to open an audio-only line to the French fleet.

"This is D...Dodgson. Sorry for the d...delay in responding, but I'm sure you can understand that we were quite n...nervous seeing a European fleet approaching."

I was surprised when an American voice came back to me. "No worries, Miss Dobson. This is Captain Peter Lane, representing the provisional government of the United States. We're working with European High Command on the peaceful transition to the new situation."

"Understood, C...captain Lane. Can I be assured that n...no-one here will be harmed?"

"As long as no-one resists European authority over the base, I can assure you that no-one will be harmed."

"It's going to be great to finally g...go home. We'll prepare the landing p...ports for you," I said cheerfully.

"I'm looking forward to meeting you, Miss Dobson." He said merrily, causing my stomach to twist inside. My lip twisted in disgust. He was a damn traitor, and no-one could doubt that. "It's D...Dodgson," I muttered darkly, as he went offline.

"That was odd..." Pentauk said softly at my side.

I glanced at her. "What was?"

"An American in command of a French vessel."

"Oh, I'm sure he's not in ch...charge. He's just a puppet for the d...damn Peons. They think it's m...more likely that we'd comply with an American, than the enemy."

"So, what now?" She asked.

"We make it look like we're g...getting ready for them to land and prepare the p...ports," I turned to Granger. "Can I trust you to see to that?"

He smiled and turned to Crystal. "See to that, would you, my dear?"

"Of course, Sir." She walked to the door to leave but faced one of my men. She glanced back at me. "With your permission, of course, Lieutenant," she said icily.

"Let her through, Baker," I said with a grin, and the Marine stepped aside. As she left, I turned around and sat in the seat next to the communications officer.

"And just what're we going to be doing?" Granger asked.

"We are going to wait. Situation report, please, Tiffany."

This time, Tiffany smiled. "I am pleased to report that the ships are once more moving toward us. With their weapons powered down."

I heard a faint beeping and looked around, but I couldn't tell where it was coming from. I tried to ignore it. "How long before they enter the range I specified?"

"Approximately thirty minutes."

The beeping behind me got louder, and suddenly became a long, ongoing tone. I stood up and turned around trying to find the source. But still, the sound was behind me. "What is that annoying noise?"

"Oh, that's the portable M.E.T.," Tiffany replied casually, not even looking over from her console, where she continued to monitor the progress of the Peons. "It was warning you that the power was low. Not bad going, seeing as it's been nearly three hours. Much longer than expected."

I quickly pulled the M.E.T. device from the back of my belt. It was indeed where the tone was coming from.

I looked up at Tiffany, confused. "You said 'was'?"

Tiffany shrugged and smiled slightly. "The long tone meant the contents have lost coherence."

I looked down at the device, and then back at her. "Are you t...telling me that he's... d...dead?"

"Absolutely." She replied chirpily.

"Why d...didn't you tell me?" I responded, aghast.

Tiffany sounded bored as she shrugged again. "To be blunt with you, I didn't want him out. And also, to be completely honest, he wouldn't have cooperated with Admiral Plural. He was a pathetic little man, who always whined about the morality of our research being used for warfare."

"That wasn't your call to make. It was mine! I should have you arrested," I said angrily.

"Pfft!" She turned to me and rolled her eyes lazily. "I'm far too valuable to be wasted in a jail cell. Your Jenna Plural will want more of these devices and have me develop them further. Also, I hate to be pedantic, but it wasn't my responsibility to inform you about it. We already told you the battery only lasts two hours."

I tossed the device to Pentauk.

"See if you can find somewhere to charge that. We may need to use it again for someone else." I looked back at Tiffany as I said the last part, and she shot me a startled look.

"I can assure you, Lieutenant. It's the right decision. With the doctor's research, there's no end to the possibilities I can deliver. He would've just continued to cause problems."

I sighed, aware that she was probably right but not liking the situation all the same.

I sat down in a chair and closed my eyes. It was only then that I remembered about what had happened to Stacey Grant. Mr. Phelkar had been with her, and a knot tightened in my stomach. I would make her pay dearly if she'd let anything happen to him.

"Hold onto your seats, everyone!" Tiffany's shout drew me from my thoughts. I opened my eyes, glancing at her. "The first ship will be in range in thirty seconds. Our weapons are powering up."

"Is there any way we c...can get it on the screen?" I asked urgently.

Tiffany shook her head. "Nope. It's not like we have cameras floating out in space."

"What's happening?

"Our first gun is preparing to fire." There was a sudden boom from somewhere far within the base, and Tiffany punched the air with a whoop. "Direct hit to the underbelly of the beast! The first ship is going down. The other ships are starting their maneuver, but...." Before she could finish her sentence, two more guns bellowed out, closely followed by the third. "Three more direct hits! We've taken out three cruisers!" Tiffany laughed. "The other ships are starting to pull up and trying to back away, but not they're not fast enough."

The guns boomed out again. This time, three hits on a miss.

"The Peon ship is hailing us again." Alerted Nolan.

"Put them on speaker," I commanded.

"What the hell is going on down there?!" Captain Lane shouted. "If you don't stop at once, they'll order the utter decimation of the entire base!"

"Oh n...no, you won't," I replied cheerily. "You n...know full well that you have orders to get the research from this base. You can't d...destroy it."

"What do you hope to achieve, *girl*? If we need to, we can just sit back and wait you out, because nothing is coming here from Earth anymore, you stupid bitch."

"Sir, you are talking to an officer of the Solar Confederation. This b...base is under the direct command of Admiral Jenna P...Plural. I advise you to turn around and retreat. You are within our territory, and we take no prisoners."

"Jenna Plural?!" Lane positively spluttered out her name. "She's a damn delusional lieutenant. You're mad to be following her."

"We've already taken out almost half of their ships," Tiffany called over to me. "However, they've backed up sufficiently far enough that they're not having any problems avoiding our missiles."

"Stop firing. No p...point in wasting missiles," I commanded, and the guns fell silent. "Captain, as you and your P...Peon masters can see, you don't have a hope in hell getting n...near us."

"The Union wants this base," he responded. "And is willing to wait for it. When was your last supply run? And where is this fucking Jenna Plural? Are you expecting her to ride over the horizon and rescue you?" He suddenly stopped talking as someone relayed something to him. He cursed incoherently, and then cut the line.

"Lieutenant." Tiffany called to me. "The Peon ships are heading out at a very strange trajectory from the moon. It looks like they're leaving." I stepped over to her and looked at the scanner. And then, right on the edge, a blip appeared. The U.S.S. Constitution was still several hours out, but following them, was the entire fleet. Tiffany grinned. "She is c...coming over the horizon."

I laughed and slapped Tiffany on the back.

The celebrations for taking the Enceladus Base rivaled those of the Battle of Deep Space. The biggest difference was that it took place on the ground. Solid ground that many in the fleet hadn't stood upon in months or even years.

Several ships came down and landed with a complement of troops and technicians who secured the base. Pentauk and I went down to the docking bay when Jenna Plural's shuttle landed. There was quite a crowd gathered, all desperate to see the woman who had saved them. And I don't mean me. As she came down the shuttle ramp, I noticed that she looked over to where I now saw Stacey Grant standing, and I immediately looked around to see if I could see Mr. Phelkar, but there was no sign of him. Grant looked seriously messed up. Her face was black and blue and severely swollen. She'd certainly been put through the wringer. She probably deserved it.

Admiral Plural made her way over to her, and they spoke very briefly before the Admiral turned away and headed back towards me. I glared at Grant, but she didn't appear to notice and just turned away, heading back to her shuttle.

Just before she reached me, I saw Admiral Plural swipe something from her eye, but then she smiled at me.

"Quite an amazing job you've done here, Lieutenant Dodgson," she returned my salute, then put out a hand to shake mine.

As we approached the control center, I told her the story of what had happened. She let some of the civilians come into the room and addressed all present.

"This is another victory for the infant Solar Confederation, taking us one step closer back to Earth. Enceladus is the first of what will be many bases and colonies loyal to the cause of freedom. Let this be our capital, and the beacon of hope to those who hide in terror from their oppressors. To victory!" She raised a defiant fist into the air, and the cry to victory rang out from all around.

When Admiral Plural learned about the M.E.T. equipment, Tiffany was immediately offered a position in Helen Tracker's team and shipped out to the Constitution. Mendez and Amy were also offered positions on board the fleet. Mendez chose to remain on Enceladus, but Amy accepted. It appeared Mahoney's wish to get credit for everything was going to come true. I, however, was not going to get the gratitude that I believed I deserved, because as we returned to the U.S.S. Constitution aboard a transport shuttle, Pentauk came and sat next to me. She looked a little uncomfortable before speaking.

"You said that after this mission, we could decide whether to remain under your command or not."

I looked at her, disappointed. "From your t...tone, I'm guessing you've d...decided that you won't be."

"Yes. Let's face it, Dodgson, Mahoney got it right. You really are a fucking psycho," she said unrepentantly. "We don't feel safe or secure under your command."

I sighed.

"I did my duty to the best of my ability. I gave you a choice, and the commodore agreed," I shrugged, but inside, I was fucking angry. The mission was successful, for fuck's sake. Ungrateful little cunts. "So, what now, Sarge? Going to report me for conduct unbecoming a Marine?"

She just snorted derisively at that. "No. I've been in this game long enough to learn you don't fuck with an officer." But then she fixed her gaze hard upon me. "Dodgson. You need to get some help. You're clearly fucked up. Do it for yourself and do it for the next poor shits put under your command."

She went to say something more, but I raised my hand and shook my head. I'd had enough of her delusions about me. She sighed, rose from her chair and went back to her seat.

I looked ahead to where the pilots sat, unable to look any of them in the eye. When we landed, I remained in that position until they'd all disembarked. I only came out when I was sure they'd be clear of the docking area.

The news that Stacey Grant had allowed Mr. Phelkar to be captured by the Peons distracted me from my negative thoughts about myself and allowed me to transfer them straight on to her. Given what she'd recently wrote in that debauched chronicle, "*That Girl from Wagga*", you may think I'm unfair in my vehemence. However, he was a civilian. Thus, it was her responsibility to keep him safe.

She'd failed, and failed abysmally. This is what comes from relying on foreigners for help. The fucking Australians had already proved they didn't have what it takes to win a war.

When the news came that Stacey's sister had directly betrayed us, I knew it was more than a coincidence. There was a traitor in our midst, and it was clearly Stacefield Ellen Grant. She as much as admitted it, when she renamed the U.S.S. Los Angeles to the R.A.S. Wagga Wagga.

The Solar Confederation was American, and Jenna had said nothing about giving that up. Grant had defamed the name of a fine ship by naming it after some outback Australian shantytown.

There was only one thing to do, but I didn't yet have the opportunity to do it. She was too far away, safely ensconced aboard the Los Angeles. And yeah, I refuse to call it by the pathetic name *she* gave it. I found myself aboard the Constitution.

I had no current duty. Commodore Addison had put me on administrative leave without prejudice when she learned of my team's decision. She had questioned me long about it. She couldn't understand why after my great success, my team still wished to depart my unit. But the result was that I was without a portfolio.

Even my relationship with Helen Tracker seemed to have gone sour. She was always working and never had time for me.

One morning a couple of weeks later, I received a call to go to Admiral Plural's office,

"Hey, Dodgson," she said with a smile as I entered. She sat back in her chair, returning my salute without getting up. "I'm sorry it's taken this long for me to get in touch with you, but I only just learned what happened after your mission. I can't say that I'm happy with you for allowing them that choice, but I'm not going to leave you dangling in the wind any longer. At the insistence of my security, I'm putting together a personal bodyguard company of people I trust. Sakamoto will be in charge of that, and I want you and Abigail Thompson to join that team. Your basic job will be to keep me alive."

"That would be quite an honor, and Ma'am, thank you for having faith in me."

Although the idea of taking orders from a Jap didn't sit well with me.

"Yes, well, I think it's unnecessary, but apparently, it's expected," the Admiral said, clearly irritated at the idea. "You'll only be called to duty when I leave the Constitution. I'll return you to logistics work when you aren't performing that duty. It's really just a civilian role, but I want you to fill it until I find someone suitable to take over permanently."

"I take it there's no possibility of getting Mr. Phelkar back," I asked.

At this, she sighed and looked away from me, staring off into space for a moment, before looking back at me. "Unfortunately not, Dodgson. You're dismissed."

I'd had my fifteen minutes of fame and I became a hero of the Confederation for a while. I was even presented with a Medal of Valor, and my face was all over the TV. I've got to ashamedly admit I do think I deserved it, don't you?

I spent a couple of days settling into my new office and handling issues of the civilian craft. The day came when there was a need to transfer some supplies between the Constitution and the Los Angeles, and I took the opportunity to oversee that operation personally, using the excuse that I wanted to perform an inspection of my staff.

I took a shuttle over to the Los Angeles and left my people dealing with whatever they had to deal with, for, to be honest, I wasn't there for any inspection. I headed up towards the bridge. I didn't know how I was going to do it, and clearly, I was going to get caught doing it, but I knew that it was necessary for Michael's sake. I was surprised that I got all the way to the bridge without anyone questioning me, and I found myself standing outside Stacey Grant's quarters. I don't know how I knew she was in there. This was a darn big ship, and she could be anywhere, but somehow, I just *knew* she was behind that door.

I couldn't believe the opportunity had come so easily. My heart raced as I stepped into her quarters. To rid the world of this foul creature, Stacey Grant, would be a joy to experience. However, she didn't seem to be there. I looked around and was about to give up and leave, when I heard a gentle sobbing from the bathroom. I gently slid the door open, and there she was, resting her hands against the sink with her back to me. Making sure I didn't step into the view of the mirror, I withdrew my knife. Her body shook slightly as she continued to be wracked with sobs. Hopefully, it was regret at what she had done to Mr. Phelkar, but that wasn't going to save her. I would be quick and clean and draw it straight across her throat. She would barely feel it.

Yes, I know I am soft; I should have let her suffer the pain and indignity for her crimes, but as I got closer, my eyes dropped to the small sliver of plastic lying on the counter next to her hands. My eyes widened, and I hesitated. Then I stumbled back, quickly slipping the knife back into my belt.

There in front of me was a pregnancy test with a thin pink line showing positive. Stacey suddenly turned around and jumped with a gasp as she saw me.

"What the fuck, Dodgson?" She snapped at me as she wiped the tears from her eyes. She quickly grabbed the pregnancy test and tossed it into the trash. "You don't just walk in on a girl in the dunny."

"I'm sorry, Ma'am. I heard you, and I thought you were in some sort of distress."

She stared at me hard. "What the fuck do you want, Dodgson?"

I can't remember the excuse I made, but she either appeared to accept it or was too wrapped up in her own concerns to care. She glanced toward the trash can and then slowly looked back at me.

"I don't know what you think you saw there, or even if you did, but it's private," she said venomously. "Tell anyone, and you and I'll have a *real* big problem. You hear me, Emma?"

"Understood, Ma'am," I replied as I tried to make sense of all this.

"Good. Now fuck off." She waved her hand dismissively at me.

I nodded, and as I headed out, I felt so confused. However, by the time I made it back to my quarters, everything was so very clear. It had to be my child. It was so obvious.

Both Jenna and I had passed our D.N.A. on to dear, sweet Michael, who had then passed it on to Stacey Grant. Why should we need to suffer the pains of labor, when that useless little whore could carry it for us?

Jenna and I were going to bring forth the next generation together, and raise him to be the future of a New America. It was going to be glorious.

AWAKENING OF HANNA GRANT

By Hannah Grant

Traitor or Patriot?

Hannah Grant is the illegal GenMod sister of legendary pilot Stacey Grant but is she all that she seems? Unlike her half sister Hannah was raised in luxury as the daughter of a multi billionaire industrialist.

Genetically designed to be flawless, she is rich, beautiful and spoiled rotten. The most popular girl in school she is also an unrepentant bully who stamps her authority on everyone around her. She has expensive luxury cars, chauffer driven limousines and the captain of the football team as a boyfriend. She has the life most of us can only dream of and stands to inherit her mother's corporate empire. Life is as perfect as her DNA. That all comes crashing down when the Peons invade her country and she watches Melbourne burn. Her life of leisure now becomes a fight to survive ...

With money now valueless and her influence gone can the little princess make in a world at war and the odds against her?

The time has come for the ...
Awakening of Hannah Grant

www.ingramcontent.com/pod-product-compliance
Lightning Source LLC
Chambersburg PA
CBHW020824260626
47169CB00003B/814